RAIDER PLAYS WITH FIRE.

The first lantern hit the top of the cross that Raider had been tied on. It broke, sending oil down to the pile of wood. No flame, though. Maybe it wouldn't work. Maybe Starbin had been . . .

A second lantern burst and the fire spread down the line of oil.

The kindling caught with ease.

Raider felt the heat rising almost immediately.

His head began to spin, his eyes went dry.

The flames licked the bottoms of his boots.

This was it. The last ride. One more way to die. Only this time he was really heading for Hell.

Other books in the RAIDER series by
J. D. HARDIN

RAIDER
SIXGUN CIRCUS
THE YUMA ROUNDUP
THE GUNS OF EL DORADO
THIRST FOR VENGEANCE
DEATH'S DEAL
VENGEANCE RIDE
CHEYENNE FRAUD
THE GULF PIRATES
TIMBER WAR
SILVER CITY AMBUSH
THE NORTHWEST RAILROAD WAR
THE MADMAN'S BLADE
WOLF CREEK FEUD
BAJA DIABLO
STAGECOACH RANSOM
RIVERBOAT GOLD
WILDERNESS MANHUNT
SINS OF THE GUNSLINGER
BLACK HILLS TRACKDOWN
GUNFIGHTER'S SHOWDOWN
THE ANDERSON VALLEY SHOOT-OUT
BADLANDS PATROL
THE YELLOWSTONE THIEVES
THE ARKANSAS HELLRIDER
BORDER WAR

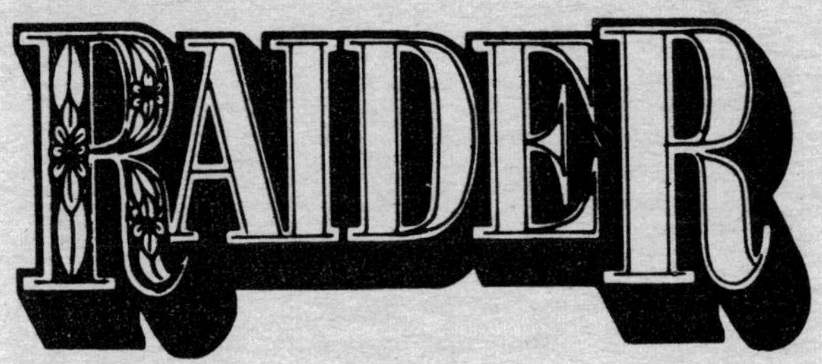

THE EAST TEXAS DECEPTION

BERKLEY BOOKS, NEW YORK

THE EAST TEXAS DECEPTION

A Berkley Book/published by arrangement with the author

PRINTING HISTORY
Berkley edition/September 1989

For information address: The Berkley Publishing Group, 200 Madison Avenue, New York, NY 10016.

ISBN: 0-425-11749-9

A BERKLEY BOOK ® TM 757,375
Berkley Books are published by the Berkley Publishing Group, 200 Madison Avenue, New York, NY 10016
The name "BERKLEY" and the "B" logo are trademarks belonging to the Berkley Publishing Corporation.

PRINTED IN THE UNITED STATES OF AMERICA

10 9 8 7 6 5 4 3 2 1

This book is dedicated to the memory of the late **Tim Donahue.** *He checked out a little early, but he had seen most of it anyway.*

CHAPTER ONE

Raider's gray gelding snorted in the night wind, plodding slowly away from the howling force that swept down the line of the Rockies behind him. The big man in the saddle didn't have to look over his shoulder for a fix on the wicked November sky. He knew he was heading southeast; he just wasn't sure of his exact location, something that could only be determined if he hit a town or a familiar landmark. Neither of those things seemed to be coming up on Lady Fortune's spinning wheel, at least not for the tall, black-eyed Pinkerton.

November could be tricky on the plains. Snow came up quickly sometimes, burying you hip deep in cold, white mush. The most frigid air known to man and God knifed right through a shearling coat or a heavy fur. Raider had on every piece of clothing he owned, including his extra blanket and his rain slicker. And still the wind bit through his denim pants, chewing right down to the ends of his Justin boots.

He wondered if the gray would make it. The animal had held up all the way from Idaho. Raider had started chasing Johnny Waco in October, picking up the trail outside Nampa. Waco had chosen to rob the wrong payroll company, one that could afford to pay a Pinkerton's wages until the tinhorn kid was found. Some said that Waco carried a gun, but no one had ever seen him use it. Raider knew little more about the outlaw, other than a detailed description that had held up for almost two months: lanky, friendly, fuzzy yellow beard, thin hair on top, although he had a young face.

Waco talked too, to anyone he met along the way. He had confessed to a prospector that he was heading for Texas, to see his family near Austin. Raider wondered if the kid had tried to salt a false trail, but he soon found Waco's course to be true and unwavering. Last seen in Boulder, four days ago, before the hellishly cold weather set in.

"Not a good night for ridin'," the big man said to the gray.

The horse snorted and nodded.

Raider pulled his arms tight under the blanket. He felt the cold iron of his Colt against the elbow of his gunhand. Best not to forget that he was chasing one that had done wrong. Even a friendly kid could get off a lucky shot.

His leg brushed the butt of the Winchester rifle that hung on the sling ring of his saddle. The cold wouldn't affect its mechanism. It was oiled and clean, ready to go . . . if Raider didn't freeze to death first.

Feeling a little guilty about riding the gray so hard, he got down to walk for a while. But he was so weary and cold that soon he climbed into the saddle again and told the gray to die first. Much to his amazement, the gray kept on going. And the wind kept on raging.

Raider forced himself to think about Johnny Waco. The kid had been smart. An inside job. Nobody even realized the gold was missing until they got the wagon up to the mines. By then, Waco had a week's head start. When Raider found his trail, it was already two weeks old. He had spoken to a tinker outside Boulder who had placed Waco two days ahead of him. The big man from Arkansas managed to shave twelve days off the trail before the cold weather slowed him down.

At least it wasn't snowing yet.

Raider cringed. He had let himself think it so now it was going to happen. The clouds were building up behind him, boiling down from the north with the wind. It didn't come right away, but it came, drifting down in light flakes that stuck like wet icing from a widow's cake.

"You gonna die?" he asked the horse.

No snort this time. Maybe the animal was near the end. Still, it just moved on, as if it thought it could escape the wind by going far enough south.

The high plains stretched out before him. Raider figured he was in the southeastern corner of Colorado, or maybe he had already strayed into Texas or Oklahoma. He kicked himself for not stopping in Denver or Boulder to trade for another horse. Killing the gray wasn't going to do either one of them any good. He needed a town. He wished for a town.

But he got snow instead.

Like a man running out of hopes, he started wishing for less and less. He wished for a house, just a sodbuster's hut. Then he would have settled for a sooner's wagon. Or an Indian tepee. Or maybe the dirtiest tarp of a skins dealer. Anything was better than rocking against the snow in a saddle.

The gray made a strange sound.

Raider lifted his eyes quickly. He thought he saw a light for several seconds, but then it was gone. A mirage. You could think up a lot of things if you got cold and crazy enough. He had heard a mountain man describing what it was like to freeze to death. Like pulling a warm blanket over you and settling into a feather bed. Raider had never bothered to ask the man how he knew what it was like to freeze to death. He figured the answer probably would have been a lie anyway.

The ground sloped downward into a snowy trough. Raider expected the animal to collapse at any moment, but instead, it started back up an incline like it was as fresh as a colt. At the top of the rise, Raider saw the light again.

"Two Buttes," he said to himself.

He was still in Colorado.

The gelding flew down the other side of the ridge, making for a second rise in the distance. The light disappeared again, but this time Raider knew why; he was on lower ground and Two Buttes was behind the far ridge. He suddenly felt warm all over. Maybe Two Buttes was the kind of place where a man like Johnny Waco would take a break from the cold weather. Maybe he was hunkered down next to a fire right now.

Raider decided he would settle for a fire and a shot of hot applejack. When he was thawed out, he'd worry about Johnny Waco. Until then, he just wanted to be able to feel his feet.

Raider eased the gray up the lone street of the one-horse town. The sign on the general store confirmed his suspicions: Two Buttes Grain and Livery. But the light wasn't burning there, so he trudged on toward the saloon. He often wondered how such places grew up. A few sodbusters would lay down roots and a town would blossom like a wart on a razorback's snout.

The saloon was lit up, but the door was locked. Raider stepped back a little and looked toward a window on the second story. A light burned aloft. The barkeeper was no doubt counting his receipts for the day. Raider was searching for a pebble to toss at the window when he heard the voice. At first he thought it was the wind, but after the words formed in his head, he looked toward another lonely structure that rose up against the snow.

"Hey, cowboy, over here."

Raider saw the woman waving to him. He lowered his hand to the cold handle of his Colt. Trailing the gray behind him, he started toward the woman's voice. Best not to trust her until he found out who she had hiding in there with her.

She had a jolly round face and dark hair and darker eyes. She spoke through the crack of a window, fighting the cold air.

"Come on up!" she cried.

Raider shook his head. "I gotta get this horse stabled."

She grimaced. "Oh, all right. Just put him in over at the general store. Around back. The storekeeper won't mind. You can pay him in the morning."

Raider nodded and started back for the general store. He eased into the barn with his Colt drawn. Maybe Johnny Waco waited in those dim recesses. But he was greeted only by the cheerful whinnying of horses who thought it was feeding time. Raider struck a match and cupped it in his hands until he found the lantern. He hovered around its warmth for a while before he started on the gelding. He wasn't anxious to get back out into the snow.

The big man hadn't groomed a horse in a long time. He usually paid other people to do it while he was hanging his black Stetson on the bedpost of the nearest whorehouse. But on this cold night, he took pains with the animal, even rubbing down its legs with a blanket.

"You done good, boy," he said, patting the gray's neck.

He was slipping the oat bag over the gelding's ears when he heard the crunching of footsteps in the fresh November snow.

His hand came up with his gun cocked and ready. "Don't move," he said as the door cracked open.

"Well I ain't standin' out here in this mess," the woman's voice cried.

She slid into the stable, smiling at him. She wore a fur coat around her thick body, Indian boots, and a fur bonnet covered her head.

"Early winter," she offered.

Raider kept the gun in hand. "Where is he?"

She frowned. "Name's Becky," she replied. "And I don't know who *he* is."

"Johnny Waco. I'm lookin' for 'im."

She shrugged. "Well, you ain't gonna find him tonight. Not in this snow."

Raider glared at her with narrow eyes. "Why was you watchin' the street?"

Becky waved him off nonchalantly. "Oh, I always keep an eye peeled on the street. You never know who's gonna ride through on a cold night. Maybe some cowboy wantin' company after the saloon's closed."

He nodded. "So, it's like *that*."

"Hey, are you the law?"

Raider shook his head. "No. But I am lookin' for a man that robbed a payroll. You got any law in this town?"

"We got a notary."

Raider wasn't sure what a notary was, but he decided it could wait till morning. He had ridden into something lucky and it was best not to mess it up. Of course, he would have to give the woman's place a good search to make sure Johnny Waco wasn't hiding somewhere.

"What's this gonna cost me?" he asked.

She winked. "Dollar a inch and two bits for breakfast."

Raider frowned. "Damn, I don't think I got twelve dollars."

She bit her cold, thick lower lip. "Well, then maybe just the two bits for breakfast will be enough."

CHAPTER TWO

The banshee wind howled off Lake Michigan, rattling the Fifth Avenue windows of the Pinkerton National Detective Agency. A lone gas lamp burned inside the office, which was all but deserted, save for two masculine figures that huddled next to a potbellied stove. Allan Pinkerton and William Wagner often stayed late at night to finish up their paper work, but tonight was a special occasion. They were expecting a visitor from the south, an important man with an important mission for the agency.

Wagner, clad in a fine winter suit, reached for the coffeepot on the stove. "He did say the train would be in at nine o'clock."

Pinkerton nodded. "Yes. But you know how it can be, William. I hear tell it's already snowing on the plains."

Wagner lifted the steaming cup toward his lips. "Enough to stop a train?"

The big Scotsman shrugged. "Who can say? Are you in a hurry to be getting home?"

Wagner thought about it and shook his head. "Not really."

He had no reason to want to brave the Chicago wind, not even if it meant heading home. On nights like this he was tempted to sleep on a cot in the file room. Even the bravest hansom cab driver would shudder to venture out past dark on such a devilish evening.

Pinkerton seemed to be thinking along the same lines. "What if he can't find livery at this hour?"

"We should have sent someone to the train station," Wagner replied.

Pinkerton shook his head. "The man himself said it wasn't

necessary. Although I doubt it's this cold in Texas in November."

Both men perked up at the same time, listening as a carriage rattled past the front window. It did not stop, so they settled back into their chairs. Pinkerton glanced at some papers on his desk.

Wagner raised a wary eyebrow. "Something wrong?"

Pinkerton shrugged. "No, not really. In fact, things seem to be in order. Our outstanding cases are fine and the ones that have been closed are all substantiated by reports."

Wagner could not help but smile. "Even Raider's?"

Pinkerton frowned, lifting a page of dirty parchment from his desk. "Shall I read verbatim?"

Wagner nodded. "Why not?"

Pinkerton cleared his throat. "Ahem. 'I, Raider, done found the thievin' varmint what kilt all them people in Wyoming. Some of them I took to justice to hang on the gallows. The others I had to kill because they was not obligin' to come with me. The territorial marshal will say this is true.' Hmm. The spelling seems to be correct. Probably dictated it to someone."

"Another case solved by the big brute from Arkansas. Did you get a report from the marshal?" Wagner asked.

"Aye," Pinkerton replied. "Raider only killed six men this time. I daresay that's below his average."

Wagner shook his head. "All by himself, too. I wonder what would happen if we teamed him with someone equally as forceful?"

"There is no one equally as forceful," Pinkerton snapped. "Unless you count the men he's pitted against. Raider is the last of a breed. We'd have to range far and wide to find another man so effective against the lower elements of criminal society. Speaking of the Devil, where is he?"

Wagner shrugged. "The last message I got from him is almost two months old. It came from Nampa, Idaho. He's chasing a . . ."

They both turned toward the front door. A carriage had rattled to a stop on Fifth Avenue. Knocking resounded over the howling of the wind.

Wagner hurried to the rapping.

A shivering, well-dressed figure stood on the wooden sidewalk. He was alone, save for the driver, who remained in the carriage. Wagner ushered the man into the office, offering his apologies for the rough weather.

The man shook his head. "It was warm and sunny when I left Texas. But that's of no real concern, sir."

"Wagner, William Wagner."

"I trust Mr. Pinkerton is here?"

Wagner nodded. "Yes, sir. If you'll come this way."

In Pinkerton's office, hands were shaken and warm coffee was poured for all.

When the man sat down, Wagner noticed the drawn, ashen appearance of their visitor. Someone who had not been sleeping well. A man with much on his mind.

Pinkerton leaned back in his chair, regarding the pale gentleman. "There was no need for you to come in person, Mr. Forbin. You could have stated your intentions in a letter. Not that it isn't an honor to be visited by the assistant state attorney for the great state of Texas."

Wagner echoed his boss's sympathies. "We were rather taken aback by your request to visit in person, Mr. Forbin. And when you asked that your arrival be kept a secret . . ."

"The governor himself sent me," Forbin replied. "What I have to tell you gentlemen concerns the security and well-being of my home state, as well as the very foundation of this free nation."

Wagner frowned. "What could be"

Forbin opened a black suitcase. "Listen to me before you protest too much, kind sirs. To steal from the bard himself, there's something rotten in the Lone Star state. If you will indulge me."

Wagner and Pinkerton leaned in, curiously eyeing the documents produced by the ashen attorney. At first they were patronizing, nodding at every word. But by the time Forbin had finished his discourse, they were both sweating through their suits, even in the coolness of the office.

"My God," Pinkerton said. "Are you certain of this?"

Forbin also wiped a sweaty brow. "Gentlemen, I am not certain of anything. The evidence speaks for itself. If you can read patterns, and I'm sure you can, it seems obvious at first glance. But then . . ."

Wagner waved him off. "No need to apologize, sir. As preposterous as it sounds, you've presented enough to warrant an investigation." He glanced toward Pinkerton for approval.

The big Scotsman nodded. "I agree, William. But, Mr. Forbin, you've got the Texas Rangers and the territorial marshal at your disposal. Why not send them to look into this?"

Forbin leaned back, sighing. "What you have seen before you is known only to myself and the governor. Two men in the whole state. But we fear that the involvement in this thing reaches into the very structure of our own government."

"What about the man who brought you all of this?" Wagner asked.

Forbin lowered his head. "His name was Horace Wilbur. He worked directly under me. It took him almost five months to amass this information."

"And?"

"Dead," Forbin replied. "His body was found last week. So you see, we had no choice but to look for outside help."

Pinkerton was rubbing his beard. "You've come to the right place, sir."

"I need as many men as you can spare," Forbin replied. "I'll meet with them personally and inform them of everything they need to know."

Pinkerton looked at Wagner. "How many men do we have available?"

Wagner sighed. He didn't want to say what they were both thinking. "One," he said. "At least until we find out what's really going on."

Forbin bristled. "Gentlemen, I didn't come all this way to have you tell me you can only spare one man!"

"We can spare more," Wagner replied. "It's just that . . . well, in a situation like this, one man can often find out more than a team. Look at your own investigation. Didn't Wilbur, a lone agent, discover all of this on his own?"

"He also discovered a bullet in the back!" Forbin offered.

Pinkerton took a deep breath, glaring at the man from Texas. "Mr. Forbin, if you're turning the investigation over to our agency, then you'll have to trust us to handle the situation as we see fit. Otherwise, I'll have to ask you to take your business elsewhere."

"But . . . I mean . . . my God, Mr. Pinkerton, if this is as big as we think it is, one man . . . I'm not sure . . ."

"You've come a long way," Wagner said in a soothing voice. "Perhaps you should sleep on it and then make a decision."

Forbin sighed deeply. "No. The governor has instructed me to trust this matter to the Pinkerton National Detective Agency. I'll abide by your judgment and your expertise. But if you're unsuccessful . . ."

"We won't be," Wagner replied. "Perhaps you should find your hotel, Mr. Forbin. It is a rather ungodly night to be . . ."

"I'm leaving in two hours on a southbound train," Forbin replied. "You have my address in Austin. Have your man report to me as soon as possible."

He stood up quickly.

"Good night, gentlemen. The fate of Texas is in your hands."

Wagner ushered him to the door and went back into Pinkerton's office.

Pinkerton was staring at the big map on the wall behind his desk. "Do you think the assistant state attorney has a case, William?"

Wagner nodded. "I do."

They were both thinking it, but neither one of them wanted to be the first to say it.

"Perhaps we should send Stokes," Wagner offered weakly.

Pinkerton nodded. "Yes, Stokes would do fine."

Wagner frowned. "You think he's capable of solving this case?"

"No," Pinkerton replied. "I think he's capable of finding Raider."

Wagner agreed. The big man from Arkansas was the only one to send into east Texas. And God help Raider if he stumbled along the way.

CHAPTER THREE

Raider eased open the door to the woman's place, staying clear of the threshold, half-expecting some sort of ambush. When the anticipated gunshot did not come, he motioned with the barrel of his colt, bidding the woman to enter first. She only huffed with exasperation and stormed past him, wheeling with an accusatory look once she was inside.

"See," she said angrily. "There's nobody here. Just me . . . and you, if you'll ever come in."

Raider held tight to the butt of his gun. He had followed her through the snow and up the wooden stairs. But he was going to make damned sure before he followed her into the small apartment.

"Step back," he said. "Open the door wider."

"My name's Becky!" she railed. "Can't you call me by my name?"

"Open the door wider . . . Becky. Go on, all the way."

She snuffled indignantly, but she still did as he said.

Raider leaned forward a little, peeking through the crack of the door to make sure no one was hiding behind it. The room was lit by a single oil lamp that had been turned low. Raider asked for more light and Becky gave it to him. There was nobody lurking behind the door.

"I'm startin' to lose patience!" she warned.

Raider's huge frame filled the doorway. "When you're in my line o' work, lady, you can't be too careful."

"And what kind of work is that? What makes you sneakier than an old alley cat?"

He ignored her anger. "Look, I wanna stay the night, but I gotta make sure I'm safe."

She motioned broadly, a gesture that encompassed her modest digs. "One room," she said. "Used to be a stable downstairs, before the livery moved over behind the general store. The farrier couldn't make it in this small town. Had to move on."

Raider saw the room clearly for the first time. Not much to it. A bed, a woodstove, a dresser, and a tattered rug over the wooden floor. Of course, there were the usual curtains and doilies that women always used to make a place seem fancier than it really was. At least the stove kept the place warm.

"The farrier lived here before," she offered.

Raider took one step into the hot air. "You used t' live with 'im?"

She nodded, blushing. "Yeah. He was all right. He never knew I whored before I took up with him. When he left, I decided to stay and go back to work. Don't nobody around here mind much."

"Why didn't you go with him?" the big man asked.

Becky shrugged. "Just didn't want to. Figured to take my chances here, by myself."

Raider eased slowly toward the bed. "You got guts, lady."

Using his Winchester, he prodded the space beneath the bed, trying to root out any would-be assailants. But there was nothing there. Only a ball of dust that came up on the end of his rifle barrel.

"Satisfied?" Becky challenged.

Raider sighed, thinking he had been a little too much on edge. It was fatigue. He always took it slow and easy when he was beat. He needed sleep. Not too much, but enough to freshen him up, so he could get back on the trail of Johnny Waco. If he hadn't lost him already.

He leaned his rifle against the closed door. "You got any whiskey?"

Becky was in the process of taking off her fur coat. Her breasts jiggled invitingly as she unwrapped her buxom body. She raised a thick eyebrow and started to tease him.

"Whiskey costs money," she said playfully.

Raider dug into the pockets of his jeans, coming up with seven dollars in coin and scrip. "That's all I got."

She took five. "This should do it. Things are slow."

"Will this be 'nough for the livery?" Raider asked.

She put the five between her breasts. "Don't fret. I'll pay him out of my share. We help each other, the storekeeper and me. Only, don't get the wrong idea. He never visits me, if you know what I mean. Too old. Naw, it's strickly business. Here, let's take off that coat."

Raider let her undress him, down to his jeans and shirt. She hung his particulars on nails in the walls, remarking that she could wash them for him if the snow quit and the sun started shining again. She asked if he would like a cup of coffee.

Raider reminded her that he had bargained for whiskey.

Becky produced a bottle and a glass. Raider took a long pull of the red-eye, which was smooth but definitely home-made. When the hooch hit him, he wobbled a little and lowered his Colt into his holster.

"Why don't you take off that gun?" Becky insisted. "And the rest of your outfit. I can . . ."

Raider waved her off. "Not now. I gotta lay down."

She moved closer to him, putting her hands on his thick chest. "Aw, don't be shy. We could . . ."

"I cain't, honey, not till after I sleep. I'm . . ."

She pushed him away. "Ooh, you don't like me. What's the matter? Ain't I pretty enough for you?"

Raider told her that she was indeed pretty enough. He remarked that she was exactly the way he liked a woman to be; big, with plenty of curves, and sweet brown eyes. This prompted her to come close again, urging him back on the bed.

Raider's body seemed to shut down when he hit the soft mattress. He was vaguely aware that she was unbuckling his holster but suddenly it didn't seem to matter anymore. He didn't feel her hands against his crotch. He only wanted to close his eyes, to escape the snowy November night.

Raider was having a good dream for a change. He was floating in the warm air of summer, flying into a round, silky bed. The blue sky loomed cloudless overhead, promising the kind of perfect spring day that would allow a man to forget all his troubles.

The girl in the dream was one he had known before, a Chinese woman he had encountered in a San Francisco whorehouse. He remembered her as the kind of lithe, Eastern beauty who would do anything for a man without a hitch. She wouldn't complain or fuss, she'd just be there right beside you, all the way, wrapping you up like she knew the very inside of your black soul.

Raider wanted to mount her on the airy bower, but she insisted on working him with her hand. He felt a moist warmth all over his body, like she was washing him with a soft cloth. He kept telling her to lie down, to spread her legs so he could enter her. But she only laughed, working her hand down to his cock.

He had to give in. She pulled at him, massaging his scrotum. He could only lie back and take the rising agony. His prick ached as it arched for the fiery release. Her hand moved up and down, driving him crazy.

Why wouldn't she let him on top?

He had to have her.

His sap was surging, if he didn't get it in her soon . . .

He exploded in her hand.

"Jesus, cowboy, I wasn't expecting that."

Raider opened his eyes.

Becky hovered over his cock, wiping the milky residue from her skin.

Raider shook his head, wondering what the hell had happened. He was naked on the bed. Apparently Becky had been bathing him with a warm cloth. Her ministrations on his private region had caused him to erupt in his sleep.

He sat up sharply, wanting to ask her for his gun.

But she was on the bed with him, half-clad in lacy white undergarments. He could see the brown rings of her nipples underneath the silky fabric. She grinned at him, pushing her chest out.

"You like it, cowboy?"

Suddenly he felt cold and alone. "Take it off."

"Ooh, I like that even better."

She got up and undressed in the lamplight. Smooth, white skin. A few lines and wrinkles, but nothing to distract his interest. He wasn't even sure of where he was or what he had been doing. He only knew that he wanted her.

Becky leaned over, touching his cock again. "You may be out of commission for a while, but we can cuddle."

She fondled him playfully in her hand.

Raider reached for her sagging breasts, running his fingers around the tight nipples. "I ain't out of commission, honey."

She flushed red. "Damn, you wasn't lyin' about havin' a full ruler."

"You're a whore," he said. "You must have some tricks to help a fellah along. Don't you?"

She smiled slyly. "Just watch."

Her chest fell on his prick, engulfing the half-erect member with soft flesh. Raider sprang instantly to life. He hadn't seen a woman in a month and he hadn't been with one for almost ninety days.

Becky gave a little anxious moan. "I got to have that thing."

"Sit on it," the big man said. "Now."

She straddled him, guiding his prickhead to the moist crevice of her cunt. He was big but she was able to accommodate his thickness in one easy motion. Her head rolled and she began to rock the mattress.

Raider just lay back, letting her work. When he felt the familiar shiver that ran through her body, he rolled her over and got on top. Becky's tongue lolled outside her mouth. She pulled him down for a long kiss, bucking beneath him like a wild bronco.

Raider met her upward motion with hard thrusts of his own.

"Give it to me, honey," she whispered in a hoarse voice. "You can't make it too hard for Becky."

He obliged her, driving her thick body down toward the floor. The bed rattled like it was going to fall apart. But it didn't.

His second release started to rise. Becky seemed to sense the swelling inside her. She grabbed his shoulders and pulled him close.

"Not inside me, cowboy. Don't need no young uns."

Raider withdrew immediately, flopping his curved manhood against her belly. She reached for his prick, jerking him like she was milking a cow. Her fingers played in the warm, sticky effluent.

Raider started to roll off her.

"No," she said, "Let's play some more. Ain't very often I get me a *gen-you-wine* cocksman through Two Buttes."

But the big man had to clear his head.

Becky pouted for a few minutes but she returned with the cloth to clean up the proof of their efforts. "Didn't expect you to shoot while you were sleepin'," she said. "And then you come right back for another shot."

Raider grunted and asked where he was. It came back slowly—the snow, the town, Johnny Waco. He described the outlaw to Becky, who said a man matching the same description had been through Two Buttes three days ago.

The big man grimaced, pushing her hand away. "Three days? But I was only two days b'hind 'im."

Becky shrugged. "Well, you been sleepin' a whole day."

"What?"

"Yeah," she replied. "You came in night before last. Been sleepin' since. I finally decided to clean you up. Just couldn't let you lie there. Hey, you want something to eat?"

Raider leaned back defeatedly. He felt better after such a long rest, but now Johnny Waco had another day on him. A day that would have to be made up in the hateful weather.

"Is it still snowin'?" he asked.

She shook her head as she pulled on a robe. "No. It's rainin' now. The snow's all gone."

That meant the plains would be muddy, like thick soup.

Might as well face it, the big man thought to himself, Johnny Waco was probably lost. Once the kid got into Texas, there were a bunch of different routes he could take to his kin: train, steamer, stagecoach.

"Why you lookin' so sad?" Becky asked.

Raider just shook his head. "You got anythin' t' eat?"

She served him stew and cornbread in bed. After he ate, she tormented him to life again. She wanted to try things that she had never done before and she was sure Raider knew how. And he did, well into the night.

It was good, but his own effort was almost half-hearted.

As he was finally falling asleep again, he felt a twinge of self-pity. He had come a long way for nothing, covering all that ground to oversleep and lose the trail. He dreamed that night, seeing Johnny Waco ahead of him, on the horizon, just out of reach. The kid was laughing as he receded into a dark, billowing cloud.

And then Becky was there, prodding him, telling him to wake up.

Raider opened his eyes to a bright morning. "What the hell is it, woman?"

"That boy," she said. "Johnny Waco."

"What of 'im?"

"He just tied his horse in front of the saloon. Rode right up main street a few minutes ago. Looked just like you said, blond beard and all."

"Slap me," the big man said.

"What?"

"Go on, so I'll know I ain't dreamin'."

She slapped him on the cheek. The sting felt good. He was awake and rested, ready to go.

He put on his clothes and then he reached for his firearms.

CHAPTER FOUR

William Wagner was irritable in the way a man gets grouchy when his schemes are not transpiring fast enough. He sat at his desk, nervously arranging and rearranging the papers on it, watching the huge oaken door that refused to open. He wanted to see the messenger boy come through with a telegram saying that Henry Stokes had found Raider. Of course, Wagner was not even sure if the first telegram had found Henry Stokes yet.

The best laid plans of mice and men, he thought to himself.

Hadn't that come from some poem?

Doc Weatherbee, Raider's former partner, would have known the origin of the prophetic line. Wagner wished Weatherbee had never quit the service, leaving Raider to work alone. The big man from Arkansas was more dangerous without the tempering influence of a civilized partner. Indeed, Raider wouldn't even accept another ruffian as a sidekick, much less a man in a suit and derby.

Wagner exhaled disgustedly. Why was he so down on Raider? The tall, black-eyed hillbilly had come through for the agency every time. He had never failed in his pursuit of a fugitive lawbreaker.

So why be so on edge?

The nature of the case, he told himself. The facts and figures shown him by Forbin had left him wondering about sending one man to east Texas. Not that Raider hadn't handled worse—or at least close to it.

His head snapped up as the front door opened.

The messenger boy came in, shivering from the cold November air.

"Well!" Wagner cried.

The boy looked up, wondering what he had done wrong. "Just the morning mail, sir."

Wagner donned his shining spectacles. "Nothing from the telegraph office? No word from a man named Stokes?"

"No, sir. Just the . . ."

Wagner stood up. "Confound it, lad, get down to the telegraph office and wait for it."

"I just sent it out yesterday, sir, I think . . ."

"I don't pay you to think. Get moving or I'll find someone else to do your job. Do you hear me?"

As soon as the lad had fled, Wagner felt guilt and remorse. It didn't befit a good commander to get cross with an underling who was performing to the best of his abilities. It wasn't the boy's fault that the message from Stokes hadn't come back.

Wagner had sent telegrams to every station south of Kansas City and west of Omaha. Stokes had last reported from Cheyenne, but he could have been anywhere on train duty. As he was recovering from a wound, the agency had given him easy duty for a while. But now they needed him to find the big galoot from the mountains of Arkansas.

What if he never heard from Stokes?

It was that damned Forbin and his crazy tales.

Part of Wagner wanted to dismiss the evidence, which was really circumstantial. And yet . . . was the state of Texas in that much danger? After all, the great territory did support its own militia, not to mention the Rangers.

If it was allowed to go too far . . .

He debated with himself in great agony for the rest of the morning.

At lunchtime, he could not decide what to do, so he stayed at his desk, shuffling through meaningless papers, glancing frequently at the front door.

At two thirty, the messenger boy came back. He stopped when he had entered the office, casting a wary glance toward Wagner's desk. Wagner caught his gaze and motioned for him to approach.

"Just popped in, sir. I waited all morning. It's from Stokes. And there's a few others too, but I . . ."

"Good, good. I'll see that you have an extra dollar in your pay."

"A whole dollar?" the kid exclaimed, wide-eyed.

Wagner thrust out his hand. "Just give me the message from Stokes," he said a bit too loudly. "Here . . ."

Allan Pinkerton stuck his head out of his office. "William, what's all this commotion?"

Wagner held up the communiqué. "From Stokes."

"Well, open it."

Wagner quickly unfolded the paper and nodded as he read. "Well, at least we've found Henry. He's in Denver."

Pinkerton rubbed his beard, staring at the floor with squinty eyes. "Hmm, not a bad place to start looking."

Wagner gazed back at his superior. "Of course, it might take him a month to find Raider."

Pinkerton nodded. "We'll give him till the end of the week."

"And then?"

Pinkerton sighed. "And then Stokes better be ready to go to east Texas."

Wagner agreed that it was the best they could do.

He penned the reply to Denver and gave it to the messenger.

"And don't dawdle," he called as the lad left eagerly.

In his mind, he told Stokes not to dawdle finding Raider.

He took a deep breath, wishing there was a way to make things happen a whole lot faster.

CHAPTER FIVE

Raider started across the muddy street toward the saloon. He was wondering why Waco had turned back to Two Buttes, but when he was close enough to the hitching post, he saw the kid's mount favoring its right hind leg. The hoof was lifted and blood was caked in with the mud. Johnny hadn't been given a choice.

Luck had come along, even though it hadn't been luck that had cut those twelve days off the trail.

Halfway to the saloon, he cranked a cartridge into his Winchester rifle. He planned to have a look through the window before he entered, although he was pretty sure Johnny Waco didn't have any idea that a Pinkerton was about to ride down on his worthless ass.

His boots didn't make a sound as he slipped up to the window. The glass was smoky, but he could see the figures around the card table inside. He thought it was a little early for a poker game, but then again, you never knew what to expect on the plains. Men with hankerings satisfied them any time or place they got the chance.

His black eyes sized up the players by one one. He smiled when he saw the fuzzy-bearded blond kid, laughing and throwing a nickel into the pot. A low stakes game, the friendly kind.

Raider eyed the other three players. All of them were rough-looking, but he still had no reason to believe they'd back up the kid. Waco didn't know anybody in these parts—or did he?

What if there was shooting and some pain-in-the-ass innocent bystander got plugged? What if the people of Two Buttes didn't take kindly to a Pinkerton coming in and shooting up their town? They might lynch Raider.

He kept watching as the cards fell, thinking that he was being unduly cautious. The game had to break up sooner or later. Then the kid would be alone. Raider could take him quietly and watch his back at the same time.

Unless . . . he tried not to think it.

The kid was calling the cards in a high voice: "Oh, big bullet. Queen of spades. Pair of tens."

Raider hadn't played poker in a while. But no . . . it was too cute. Raider never tried anything cute. It wasn't his way.

"Pair of tens takes it!"

He watched the kid drag the pot. Cocky smile on that young face. He thought he had gotten away with a fortune and now he was gloating over winning a few nickels.

Raider was suddenly angry. Cocky punk kids brought it out in him sometimes. Kids that needed to be taught a lesson and humiliated at the same time. Tinhorn punks that deserved a comeuppance.

The tall man pushed through the saloon door, holding the Winchester on his hip. He waited for somebody to pull a gun, but no iron flashed in the dull light. The card players just gaped at him. The kid was blushing.

"What's it gonna be, stranger?" said one of the players. "You gonna shoot us or join us?"

Raider lowered the barrel of his rifle. "Hell, boys, I just thought you might use another hand at the table."

They all breathed easier when Raider offered them a coyote grin, but he glared straight at Johnny Waco.

The kid grinned and offered him a chair.

After a while, Johnny Waco stopped smiling. He was losing every hand to Raider. The others were playing along but they weren't staying in the hands like the kid and the big, black-eyed man. Raider kept one eye on Waco, making sure he didn't reach beneath the table for a pistol. No gunbelt on his hip. He probably had his iron hidden in his thick coat.

Johnny laid his cards on the table for a hand of draw. "Three sevens," he said, leering at Raider. "Can you beat it?"

"Bet he can," said one of the other players.

Raider smirked. "Drew me a baby straight, honcho. One, two, three, four, five."

He slapped the five cards face up on the table, arrogantly invoking the bad-winner attitude he had seen in other gloating men. You never gloated at the card table when you won, the same way you never got mean when you lost. A good poker player had to maintain an even temper.

Johnny Waco was starting to frown and snort. "You're dealin' yourself some good cards, mister."

Raider leaned toward him. "You gotta know when t' push your luck, kid. That's what I'm doin'. How 'bout you? You know when t' push your luck?"

The kid swallowed and edged his chair away. "Hey, don't get riled. I didn't mean nothin'." He tried to smile.

Raider put the cards in front of him. "Deal, boy."

Waco shook his head. "Don't think I want to play anymore. Lost about a dollar already."

The other players were starting to shift nervously in their chairs.

Raider gritted his teeth, flashing a hateful look in the kid's direction. "Ain't right for a man to leave a game."

"I tell you, I lost a dollar!"

"He don't have to play," one of the others offered diplomatically.

"No," said another man. "He don't have to play. Does he, Wilton?"

The barkeeper came close to the table for the first time. He was a puny, weak-faced man with worry ruts in his forehead. Wilton didn't want anyone shooting up his saloon, though it had probably happened before.

"He don't have to play, mister. Not if he don't want to." Wilton's voice was quavering. "He already lost a dollar."

"Yeah," the kid protested.

His slender hands moved for the edge of the table.

"Pick up those cards," Raider said.

The hands stopped. "I ain't playin' no more. I'm out of nickels."

"Nickels?" the big man guffawed. "We ain't playin' for nickels, Johnny. No more nickels on this table."

Waco stiffened. "How'd you know my name? I never told you my name."

"You're pushin' your luck, Johnny. Deal the cards."

The tension eased somewhat in the room when Waco dealt

out the first two cards for five-card stud. Raider showed a club ace up. The kid had a five of diamonds.

"Deal the other three cards," Raider said.

Johnny hesitated, but then dealt three up-cards while the others watched intently.

Raider kept his eyes focused on the skinny outlaw, waiting for his hands to move. "I bet a thousand dollars," he offered.

Waco froze. "I ain't got it."

"A thousand dollars," the barkeeper intoned, whistling after he said it.

"He ain't got it," said one of the onlookers.

Raider smiled like the joker of the deck. "He's got it. It's in his saddlebag under the table. Scrip an' gold. I kicked it a coupla times."

The kid didn't know which way to move. "Listen, mister," he said, his voice cracking, "this ain't funny."

"Raise you a thousand!" Raider rejoined.

"Where would a boy like this get a thousand dollars?" the barkeeper asked.

"Two thousand," Raider corrected. "An' he stole it from the Idaho Copper Comp'ny. I still don't know how he got away with it."

Johnny Waco appealed to his audience. "I swear, I don't know what this man is talkin' about."

"Don't you, Johnny Waco? Don't you know for sure that I'm the Pinkerton what's chasin' your worthless ass?"

Everybody jumped back when the movement started. Waco was fast, like a pygmy rattler. But Raider was right there, moving with him. The old razorback Pink still had a few tricks in his pocket.

Johnny went for a gun in his belt, beneath his coat.

Raider saw it like it was happening very slowly. Fingers gripping the handle of an old Navy Colt, barrel slipping out of Waco's pants. He caught the kid's wrist and stood up, spinning Johnny until he was lying facedown on the table with his arm behind his back.

The hammer of Raider's Colt rattled and cold metal pressed against Johnny Waco's skinny neck. "I'm a Pinkerton agent," Raider said. "I'm takin' this one back t' Idaho for stealin' a payroll. Anybody got any truck with that?"

They were still mesmerized by the quickness of it all.

Raider had apprehended the kid in a split second. They almost couldn't believe it.

The barkeeper came to life first. "I ain't agin you doin' your duty, big man. But how do you know this is the man you're lookin' for?"

"Yeah," the kid groaned.

Raider bounced his head off the table one time. "Wilton . . . that's you, right?"

The barkeeper nodded.

"All right. Get that saddlebag out from under the table. Go on, nobody's gonna hurt you. If this little shitbird moves a inch, I'll splatter his brains all over this deck o' cards."

Moving cautiously, the weak-faced man reached for the saddlebag on the floor. It was so heavy that he could not lift it properly. He stumbled as he backed away and the saddlebag fell out of his hands.

Their eyes widened when gold double eagles spilled out onto the floor. Raider wondered if the card players and the barkeeper would get any wild notions with that much yellow are glittering in their eyes. Many a weak man got strong in the face of unearned riches.

Best to head it off in a hurry, the big man thought.

"Don't get feisty, boys. The first one who tries, I'll lay out for the undertaker's measurin' stick."

They just kept staring at the double eagles.

Raider snarled at them. "Hey, snap outta it."

The barkeeper looked up at him. "There's so damned much!"

"It ain't our'n," Raider replied. "But look here. Wilton, an' you two boys there. Go on and pick up one twenty-dollar piece for yourself."

They frowned at Raider like it was a trick.

"It ain't our'n," one of them repeated.

"We got no right to it," the barkeeper said.

Raider nodded toward the gold. "Go on, one each. And don't think it's for free. You're gonna earn it."

"I'll tell," the kid cried. "I'll tell how you gave that gold away. You'll go to jail same as me."

Again the big man dribbled Waco's head on the table.

"Ow, that hurts."

"Go on," Raider urged. "Take one coin."

"But he's gonna tell."

"Shit, you think anybody's gonna b'lieve this peckerwood? Look it 'im. A weasel if ever there was one. Don't fret. I'll say that he spent what's missin'. Now, you want twenty dollars? Or do you want your pecker in your hand?"

They decided they wanted the twenty dollars. Raider watched to make sure they only took one coin each. The barkeeper was eager to help now.

"What you need, Pink-man?"

Raider nodded. "That's better. First, I want you to put all that loot back in Waco's saddlebags."

No sooner said than done.

"Okay, get me a rope. Plenty o' rope."

Wilton hurried to the task.

Raider eyed the other two card players. "You boys got guns?"

They nodded cheerfully.

"Bullets, too?"

They said they had bullets.

Raider frowned impatiently. "Well, go get 'em."

They left as quickly as the barkeeper.

Johnny Waco squirmed on the table. "I'm gonna tell that you gave away the payroll money, Pinkerton."

The Colt barrel dug harder into the kid's neck. "Tell all you want, Waco. Them boys in Idaho is gonna be glad t' see any o' their money back. An' the way you was throwin' them nickels 'round, all careful-like, I'm bettin' that sixty dollars is the first money spent outta that payroll."

"You so friggin' smart!"

"Save your breath, boy. You can tell me all 'bout how you pulled it off on the ride back t' Idaho."

After a few minutes, the barkeeper came back with the rope.

The two sentries were right behind him. They were carrying old single-shot rifles that looked pretty rusty. They both nodded when Raider asked them if the rifles would shoot.

"Keep a bead on 'im," the big man ordered. "I'm gonna tie 'im up."

He used the rope to lash Johnny Waco to one of the rickety chairs from the card table. The kid reluctantly sat down and took his medicine. All the fight had gone out of him.

"Trussin' him up mighty good," said one of the riflemen.

"Arms and legs and all," the barkeeper agreed. "Makin'

him sit down like that too. Boy, I guess you Pinks know your business."

"I reckon we do, Wilton."

When Johnny was completely trapped in the chair, Raider dragged him next to the window and leaned him back against the wall. He balanced the chair so Johnny would fall if he moved even a little. It was a trick he had used before, to keep a man imprisoned when there was no jail around.

Raider turned back to his new accomplices. "This is the way it lays, boys. I gotta get my horse an' square a few things over t' the gen'ral store. Then I'm comin' back here t' get fuzz-face. All you heroes have t' do is stop 'im if he tries t' move. Don't listen to nothin' he has t' say. Don't get close to 'im. Just keep those rifles handy an' earn your twenty bucks."

"I got a shotgun," the barkeeper announced triumphantly.

Raider nodded. "Git it. And don't try nothin' fancy. I'll be back in a few minutes."

He reached for the saddlebag full of gold.

"He's leavin'," Johnny cried. "He's stealin' all my money."

Raider shot a look at the barkeeper. "Like I said, don't listen t' nothin' he says. 'Cause if you let 'im go, I'm gonna take back the money I gave you."

That seemed to convince them.

The big man hefted the saddlebag and walked out of the saloon.

When Raider had squared things at the general store, he went around back to get his mount. The air was warmer now, although the November chill had not died entirely. And it was going to get colder as he rode north with the kid. Damn it all, there had to be another way to make a living. He had just never been able to find it.

He was lifting his saddle when the woman spoke.

"Gonna leave without sayin' good-bye?"

Becky was leaning against the stable door, clad in her fur.

Raider lowered the saddle. "Well, y' see, I . . ."

"I know, I know. You're the big hero. Caught that boy you was chasin'. Heard somethin' about some gold, too. You wouldn't happen to have . . ."

He gave her a double eagle. So far he had spent about a hundred dollars. How much had been stolen in the first place?

Five or six thousand. They'd never miss it. He was too tired to worry.

Becky put the double eagle between her breasts. "The way I see it, you got another ride comin', cowboy. Two or three if you need it."

Raider moaned. "Aw, honey, I cain't . . ."

Why did he suddenly have to smell her perfume?

"Long ride back to where you're goin'," she offered. "Draggin' that prisoner all the way. Hell, if a woman laid down for you right on the trail, you'd still have to keep an eye on the kid while you poked her."

Why did she suddenly have to start making sense? He remembered the times on the trail when he had ached for a woman. He grabbed the saddle and threw it on the back of the gray.

"Long time between women," she said. "And it's a pity to waste that thing you got twixt your legs."

"All right," he said, wanting to be rid of the temptation. "Go on back and I'll see you in a few minutes."

"No, right here," she said. "Right on that pile of straw."

She pushed past him, heading for the cushion of hay.

Raider gaped as she lay down, pulling the coat and her dress above her thighs. She spread her legs for him. A wry smile on her face.

Raider felt the stirring when he saw the dark patch of hair. No man could have resisted that. Best just to top her and get it over with. If he did it fast enough, his luck wouldn't change.

"Let me pull it out for you, honey."

Her hands were quick on the buttons of his fly. She stroked him a little but he didn't need much coaxing. She laughed when he fell between her legs.

Raider prodded until the head of his cock found the wet entrance of her cunt. They ground together, Raider screwing his length into her. Even in the coolness of the stable, they were able to work up a sweat.

She reminded him to pull out before he came.

Raider obliged her, depositing his milky offering on her curvy stomach.

"Ain't never gonna forget you," Becky whispered.

For a moment, he wondered if she was going to ask to come with him. Her eyes were glassy and her lips trembled slightly. He felt sorry for her, but there was no chance of dragging her along, even it meant somebody warm in his bed-roll.

"Cowboy, I . . ."

"Pinkerton!"

The call from outside allowed him to spare her feelings.

He stood up, buttoning his fly. "Yeah, what is it?"

The barkeeper was standing outside the door. "Trouble. You better come quick."

Raider wanted to blame the woman for his sudden turn of bad luck, but he knew deep down that it was his own fault for allowing himself to be distracted.

He met the barekeeper, who looked worried.

"Did Waco escape?"

"No, sir. But it's almost as bad. I don't know how to tell you. You'll have to come see it for yourself."

Raider knew that was the only thing to do.

CHAPTER SIX

Wilton, the barkeeper, almost had to run to keep up with Raider's long strides toward the saloon.

"How'd it happen?" the big man asked defeatedly. "The two rifle boys let Waco take their guns away?"

Wilton shook his head. "It all came up so quick-like."

"It always comes up quick-like."

"Could you slow down, big man?"

Raider stopped as he turned into the muddy street. He stared toward the saloon, looking for Johnny Waco. He wanted the kid to come out and face him, get it all over with in a couple of bites from his Colt's flaming bore. A fair head-on fight would have looked pretty good to him.

Wilton was frowning at his endangered establishment. "I hope he doesn't set fire to the place."

"He's still in there?" Raider asked.

The barman nodded. "See, it happened like this. Jake and Honker, them's the other two boys you was playin' cards with . . ."

"I don't need to know their family history."

"Okay, well, they was guardin' that boy as pretty as you please. I was right there with 'em, too. Had my shotgun."

Raider shook his head. "Three guns and you still let 'im get loose?"

"Warn't our fault he got free. That damned chair just gave way. Fell apart without so much as a warnin'."

"Three guns, good Lord . . ."

Wilton lowered his eyes to the ground. "Yeah, I know. But see, Jake went to get off a shot, but his gun just fizzled. Then Honker managed to let one go, only it just grazed the kid. Got him in the meaty part of his leg."

That bit of news made Raider feel a little better. "He's hit?"

"Yep. But then he starts after Honker. Honker tried to fight him off but he's got a bad arm. So the kid grabs him and gets a choke hold on him. I was aimin' my gun but I couldn't shoot old Honker."

Raider sighed disgustedly. "No, you wouldn't wanna do that."

"Anyway, Waco dragged Honker behind the bar, lookin' for a gun. I mean, he's strong for somebody so slim. Anyway, there wasn't no gun so he picked up a knife and says, 'Tell that Pinkerton he better let me go or I'm gonna slice this man's throat and then I'm gonna burn your bar down!' "

Raider pulled up the collar on his coat to ward off the wind. More snow on the way. What the hell did it matter with his present sorry state?

"Gimme that shotgun," Raider said. "An' stay here."

"Yes, sir."

With the scattergun in hand, Raider started across the street. The man named Jake was standing by the window, peering in. Raider pushed him aside and took a good look.

Johnny Waco was behind the bar, still holding the knife to Honker's throat. He must have seen Raider in the window because he cried out: "I'm gonna kill him, Pink. Then I'm gonna torch this place."

Raider turned to Jake. "Thought you said that ol' gun o' yours would shoot."

Jake blushed and looked away. "You gonna take back that money?"

Raider handed him the shotgun. "If he tries to leave, plug 'im."

"Wonder why he didn't run?" Jake asked.

"B'cause he's got a bum leg an' he knew I'd catch 'im."

He started for the general store.

Wilton fell in behind him. "What are you gonna do?"

Raider just kept silent. He found the storekeeper alone behind his counter. Not a bad sort of man, a notary, whatever that was. He peered hopefully at Raider, like he expected the big man to spend some more money.

"What can I do for you, sir?"

"You got any dynamite?"

Wilton almost fainted. "No, you ain't gonna blow up my place! I put too much in that to . . ."

"Shut up, Wilton."

The storekeeper's smile had vanished. "Dynamite?"

"You got it or ain't you?"

"He's gonna blow up my bar," Wilton continued. "He's . . ."

Raider didn't want to cuff him, but he figured it was the easiest way to shut him up. Wilton was almost hysterical now and he had no intention of cooperating in the proceedings. It wasn't a hard punch, but it was well aimed, straight for the point of the chin.

The storekeeper looked over the counter at the sleeping man. "Hmm. Nice shot. Right on the button."

Raider acted like nothing had happened. "Ain't got time for dawdlin', pardner. What's the story on some red thunder?"

The man shook his head, rubbing his stubbled chin. "Well, I reckon I have to say yes and no."

"Come again?"

"Well, about a year ago a man came to order some dynamite, but he never came back to claim it. Ordered a bunch of fuse too. 'Course, I been sellin' it a stick at time, with the fuse."

"Just show me what you got."

As the man disappeared into the back of the store, Raider went to the window for a look. Jake was still at his post, holding the shotgun. The big man thought about just going in and shooting the hell out of the kid. But that might mean plugging Honker. And hell, he had played poker with Honker after all.

"Here you go, cowboy."

The storekeeper set a wooden box down on the counter. A big coil of fuse lay at the bottom of the box, but there was only one small half stick of red dynamite left. Raider wondered if it would be enough.

"That gonna suit you?" the storekeeper asked.

"How much?"

He waved the big man away. "On the house."

"I'm gonna need some other things," Raider said.

"Name it. Bullets, rope. If I got it, it's yours. 'Course, I'll have to charge you for it."

The man's jaw dropped when Raider asked him for an old broom handle and a bucket of red paint.

• • •

Johnny Waco's humiliation was almost final. Raider had set it all up, much to the astonishment of Jake and Wilton, who wondered what the hell he was doing. Wilton had recovered from the knockout blow and was keeping his mouth shut to avoid further punishment.

"Sorry I had to clock you," Raider said to the weak-faced man. "You can both keep your money no matter what happens."

Jake thanked Raider, but the barkeeper was still uncertain.

"Don't worry, Wilton. I ain't gonna blow up nothin'. You'll see."

He picked up the bundle of red sticks and started toward the saloon.

Johnny Waco was still behind the bar, holding the knife to Honker's throat. Raider stepped up to the window, peering in. The kid saw him again.

"You hear me, Pink? I mean it. Are you gonna let me go?"

Raider replied, "Sure, I'm gonna let you go, Johnny."

For a moment, the kid was silent. Then: "What?"

Raider held up the fake bundle of red shafts so the kid could see it plainly through the window. "Dynamite, Johnny. I'm gonna let you go all the way t' heaven."

"You son of a bitch!"

"You said you were gonna burn down the place," the big man challenged. "I thought I'd save you the trouble."

"What about this yahoo?"

Raider shrugged. "Honker don't mean nothin' t' me. Just another barfly. B'sides, you'll have somebody t' travel with you when you head up t' St. Peter's door t' knock."

A nervous chortle from the kid. "Aw, that dynamite ain't real."

Raider was waiting for him to say something like that. He took a match out of his coat pocket and torched the end of the fuse on the real half-stick of dynamite. He let Johnny see the sparkling fuse and then tossed the stick into the street. The explosion was louder than Raider had figured. It took a few windows with it and left a crater in the street. Mud rained down for several seconds after the blast.

Raider looked back through the smoky glass, which had somehow survived. "That real enough for you, Johnny?"

"You crazy bastard!"

"I'm gonna put these charges all 'round the saloon,

Johnny." He held up the long coil of fuse. "Then I'm gonna wire it all t'gether an' light it. I'd say you have 'bout five minutes t' live. Better start makin' your peace with the man upstairs."

Johnny Waco was suddenly interested in other alternatives. "Wait, big man. Don't. Please."

"Come along peaceable an' you won't get killed," Raider offered.

"They'll hang me in Idaho."

Raider shook his head. "No they won't. They don't hang men up there for just stealin'. You'll be in prison a long time, but they won't hang you."

Of course, Raider knew this wasn't entirely true, but he figured the kid had to take his chance with a judge and jury.

A cry of anguish from inside the saloon. Johnny Waco had pushed Honker aside. He was fleeing toward the back of the bar, no doubt looking for a rear exit. Raider stepped alongside the building, heading for the back door.

Johnny was already out and running when Raider got there. The kid was limping on his wounded leg. Raider fired his Colt into the air and the kid came to a quick stop. He turned to face the big man with crazy eyes.

Raider lowered the Colt at the middle of Waco's chest. "You got two choices, boy. Come alive or come dead. Either way you'll be ridin' sideways 'cross a hoss. Jus' say the word."

Johnny Waco collapsed into the mud, crying. "Alive," he muttered.

Raider gathered him up and took him back to the general store. The storekeeper bandaged the kid's wound while Raider looked on. When Waco was able to stand up again, Raider had to bargain for a fresh horse. After all, the kid's mount was lame now. He took the money out of the payroll stash.

Johnny Waco eyed the saddlebag. "You're spendin' more of that than I did."

"One more word outta you, boy, an' I'll gag you."

Waco lowered his head and cried some more.

Somehow, the big man could not feel sorry for him.

"So, the big hero, twice in one day!"

Becky came through the doorway with a possum smile on her thick lips.

Raider waved her off. "No more."

"You're not even tempted?" she asked.

He was tempted a little, but he shook his head. She had been a good time, but he had to get back to business. Best just to put Two Buttes behind him. Get the hell out and never look back.

CHAPTER SEVEN

Two days after the apprehension of Johnny Waco, the going was still slow. Rain had replaced the November snow, and the wind stayed steady and cold. Raider had left Two Buttes with the kid lying belly-down on the saddle of a black mare. But when the chill bit into them, he let the kid ride upright, keeping his hands tied. He even let him have an old, tattered rain slicker that had been wadded up in the bottom of his saddlebag.

Johnny bewailed his woes like many wrongdoers who found it easy to be penitent after they were caught. He complained about riding at night, especially when he saw the lights of Denver glowing against the stormy sky. Raider just ignored him, wondering if he had enough strength to get the kid back to Idaho. He was getting too old for traipsing around in the desolate, god-forsaken wilderness.

"Why can't we go to Denver?" Johnny asked. "I ain't never been there before."

"Shoulda gone when you was a free man," Raider replied.

Four days into the ride, the weather broke a little. The rain stopped and the sun came out, even though it remained cold. Raider eased up for the first time, stopping to make camp that night. Johnny Waco wondered why the big man kept looking back over his shoulder, but he had learned enough about Raider to know he wasn't the talking kind.

Their encampment rested in a natural windbreak between five large boulders. Raider managed to find enough wood to make a small fire. He also shot a wounded mule deer, a small spike buck that had survived an attack by some kind of predatory animal. The fire was barely hot enough to roast a few small pieces which they ate almost raw.

Still, the warmth and the repast were enough to make Johnny remark that the whole thing was better "than a poke in the eye with a sharp stick."

Raider sat across from the kid, staring at him.

"Whatchoo lookin' at?" Waco snarled.

Raider laughed. "Not much. How'd a boy like you ever get into robbin' an' thievin'?"

Johnny lowered his head and for a minute the big man thought he was going to cry. But he looked up again, starting to wail in a sharp voice: "That payroll was the only thing I ever took."

Raider got up, reaching for another small stick of wood. He tossed it on the fire and stood there staring into the flames. His head popped up after a few moments and he listened to the wind.

Johnny didn't seem to notice. "Yeah, I was the bookkeeper for that mining company for almost a year. Didn't pay me much, but I was loyal. Then one day they come to me and said I wasn't goin' to work for them much longer. That's when I got the idea to steal the money."

Raider looked back into the flames. "I'm wonderin' how you pulled that off." He raised his head again, listening.

Johnny went on in a prideless voice. "Oh, it wasn't that hard. Every month it was the same. The Wells Fargo box would arrive and I'd go get one of the other office boys to help me crate it up in a big box, so's they could take it on up to the mines."

He sighed, shaking his head. "I thought it was going to be so easy. I just took all the gold and scrip and put lead in the strongbox. Then I crated it up and put it on the wagon. The two shotgun guards never had any idea that they didn't have the real thing. That night, I loaded up and started off by my lonesome. Headin' back to Texas."

The wind howled around the boulders, stirring the embers of the fire.

"I'm from Texas," the kid went on. "Waco, Texas. That's why they started callin' me Johnny Waco. Real name's Newbitt Johnson. Johnny Waco was the first nickname I ever had. I reckon Raider is a monicker for . . ."

He looked up to see that Raider was no longer there.

"Pinkerton?"

The wind gave him a bitter reply.

"Where the hell did you go?"

No reply from the deep shadows.

Johnny mused for a few minutes before he decided to seize the moment at hand. With Raider gone, it was probably his only chance for escape. Why the hell had the Pink left, anyway? Were they about to be attacked by bandits or renegade Indians?

The kid decided it was better not to think about it. He began to squirm, trying to wriggle out of his ropes until he heard soft footsteps. He looked up, expecting to see Raider standing over him.

"Hey, I wasn't tryin' to . . ."

But it wasn't Raider. Instead, a smallish, potbellied man slid up next to the fire. He wore a bowler derby and several layers of clothing hidden beneath a wool coat. He had short, stubby hands, a reddish face, and a crooked nose. His expression seemed almost apologetic.

"Looks like you're fit to be tied," he said in a voice that smacked of a Georgia drawl. "Mind if I sit by this fire?"

Waco wasn't sure what to do. He smiled hopefully. "Hey, good thing you come along, mister. I was just about to be killed by a gang of thieves. Tied me up here and left me for dead. Maybe you could untie me."

The stranger ignored his plea. "Sometimes a man is tied up for a good reason," he said. "That why you're tied up? A good reason?"

"Honest Injun," Waco replied, "I was set upon by a band of outlaws. Why, only your arrival scared them off."

The round little man pushed back his hat and shook his head. "Dang me if I ain't a whole lot scarier than I thought. I mean, my mere presence caused a whole band of men to up and run off. I must be gettin' a mite ugly in my old age. Hell, they probably thought I was a sawed-off Sasquatch."

"Ain't right to make fun of a God-fearin' man what's fallen on hard times, mister."

The stranger took a long look at him. "Yeah, you seem the God-fearin' kind. You're just lyin' there fearin' the hell out of the almighty. I want to be the first to say it looks good on you, too. Why, if I was you, I'd have the good Lord himself come down here an' untie me. I bet He can't wait to take a soul like you into His glorious bosom."

Waco snarled at the intruder. "You son of a bitch. Cut me loose right now, or I'll . . ."

"Tsk, tsk. Seems to me you ain't in no position to make any threats, boy. I'm the one whose hands are free."

Suddenly it occurred to Waco that the small man might do him harm. "Hey, I'm sorry, mister. I'd be obliged if you'd set me free. I mean, don't hurt me or nothin'. I wasn't meanin' no disrespect, but when it comes to my troubles, you don't know the half of it."

The stranger hunkered by the fire, warming his hands. "Maybe not. Unlessin' you'd be the one called Newbitt Johnson, alias Johnny Waco."

The kid gaped at him. "What the hell . . ."

"Wanted for payroll thievery in Idaho," the stranger said. "On your way back there now with a boy name of Raider. Huh? Am I right?"

An expression of disbelief told the stranger he had hit the nail squarely. "That's what I thought. You're Waco. And if I ain't missed my other guess, ol' Raider's sneakin' up on me right about now!"

The stranger whirled with a quickness that belied his overgrown-bear-cub form. A large-caliber derringer had appeared as if by magic in his stubby hand. He held it on the six-foot two-inch cowboy who was aiming the Winchester at him in a Rocky Mountain standoff.

"Kill him," Johnny Waco cried. "Kill that Pinkerton son of a bitch."

The stranger started to laugh as Raider stepped into the circle of fire light. "Not bad, Raider. You're sneaky as ever."

The big man laughed too. "Hell, Stokes, it's good t' see you. I'd shake that stump you call a hand if you wasn't holdin' that peashooter in it."

"I reckon you heard me comin'," Henry Stokes replied.

"Since this afternoon. How the hell you find me?"

They both hunkered down by the fire.

"I'd just about give up," Stokes said. "If I hadn't found you by tonight, I was supposed to wire the office and tell them."

Johnny Waco was rocking back and forth, moaning. "Damn it all, if it wasn't bad enough that I had to be caught by one Pinkerton, now I got me two."

Stokes shook his head, smirking at the outlaw. "They always get sorry after they're tied up."

"Aw, don't pay no 'tention t' him," Raider said. "How'd you pick up my trail?"

"Well, I was in Denver," Stokes replied. "When word came that I was supposed to find you, I headed north. Only I soon found out that you was headin' south. So I doubled back. Stroke of luck that I spotted this campfire. 'Course, you and me always was the luckiest bastards on the face of this earth, big 'un."

Raider nodded appreciatively. Looking at the runty, chubby little man, you'd never know Stokes was one of the best agents working for the Pinkerton Agency. Raider had always thought of Henry as a badger, rooting out things where nobody else would go or could go. He had never worked with Stokes, but he had respect for him and knew one or two of his favorite habits.

"You still carry that bottle o' corn squeezin's?" the big man asked.

"Got my horse tied just over there."

"Well, go on, Henry!"

Stokes took a deep breath and exhaled slowly. "Raider, this ain't a social call. The old man wants you . . ."

"After we drink," Raider said. "It's the best time t' talk."

The fire had been bolstered by a few dung chips that Stokes had brought along in his saddlebags. Stokes was like that. He always seemed to be ready for anything. In many ways, the grunty agent reminded Raider of his former partner, Doc Weatherbee. Only Stokes was more down to earth.

Henry offered him the jug of corn liquor. "They want you down in Texas, Raider. They said you should get to Austin as soon as you can. Report to a man named Forbin in the state attorney's office. Sounds like big doin's."

"It usually is." Raider scoffed, shaking his head, swallowing another mouthful of the burning liquid. "Hell, Henry, it's prob'ly 'nother chicken pickin' job."

"I don't know," Stokes said cautiously. "This sounds like some real shit, big 'un. Otherwise they wouldn't have sent me to look for you."

Raider nodded. "Might be somethin' in that."

"Give me back my jug."

Raider looked at the pitiful shape of the kid. "What about Waco there?"

Stokes shrugged. "Aw, we could just shoot him."

Johnny whined, "No! Please!"

"He ain't gonna shoot you," Raider said.

Stokes laughed. "Boy, they get mightily in love with life after they know that rope's gonna be wrapped around their neck."

"They ain't gonna hang me," Johnny said weakly.

"Who told you that?"

Johnny nodded at Raider.

Raider winked at Stokes.

"Oh yeah," Stokes said, winking back. "I reckon they stopped all that hangin' up in Idaho. I was thinkin' about Montana."

Raider sat still for a while, thinking. He really didn't want to beg off the payroll case, not until Johnny and the money were delivered to the marshal in Boise. Of course, if he was going to give up the prisoner, he was glad that Stokes was there to take him back. Still, it was bad luck to quit in the middle of a case. He had never done it before.

"Texas, huh?" he said finally.

Stokes nodded. "Lot warmer down there. Besides, if you don't do like you're ordered, they'll come down on both of us. Hell, we might even lose our jobs."

"Gotta have another drink," the big man offered. "Don't hawg that jug, Henry."

"Never was one to hoard whiskey."

A few more pulls of the liquor put things in perspective. They even let Johnny Waco have a slug. The kid coughed and wheezed and spit most of it out. He said the peckerwood Pinks were already trying to kill him.

Raider looked at Stokes, who was smiling. "You gonna be able t' listen t' that mouth all the way back t' Idaho?"

Stokes shrugged. "Don't know. Might have to sell him to the Sioux, what's left of him."

Johnny lowered his head and started to cry.

"I know just how you feel, son," Stokes offered.

"Texas, huh?" Raider repeated.

"Get goin', big man. You know it's the right thing to do."

Raider said he'd get started the first thing in the morning.

CHAPTER EIGHT

William Wagner had kept busy all day, trying not to think of the main quandary that plagued his darker thoughts.

Like a man set on forgetting a death in the family, he pored over his papers, paying way too much attention to niggling details that really wouldn't have mattered on a better day. He sharpened his quill pen until the point was capable of scrawling the thinnest black line. Several times before each word was written, he stirred his inkwell compulsively, making sure that any sediments on the bottom were subsequently dispatched to thicken the ink.

He kept at his papers, never looking up to see who had come through the front door of the agency. Wagner was playing a game with himself, trying to ignore the messenger boys as if the neglect would bring the message from Stokes that much faster.

Still, the cold day wore on with no word from Stokes or Raider. The deadline for Stokes's own message had passed three days ago, which under normal procedure would not be that unusual. Telegraph wires were constantly being blown down by storms or vandalized by renegades and outlaws. Stokes may have already sent the wire only to have it reach a snag on the way to Chicago. Why, the very communiqué he had been waiting for could be sitting on the desk of some key operator who simply was waiting for the line to be restored up the road. Or maybe Stokes had . . .

"Sir?"

He looked up to see the messenger boy he had berated a few days before. "What is it, lad?"

"A message from Texas."

Wagner took a deep breath to fight off the burning that had

appeared so suddenly in his chest. "Well, give it to me then."

"Yes, sir. And thanks for that extra dollar on Friday, sir. I needed it for my mother. She's . . ."

"Yes, yes," Wagner replied, opening the envelope. "If this is what I've been waiting for, you'll have another fifty cents in your next pay voucher."

"Gee, thanks . . ."

The boy watched as Wagner read the message:

CANNOT WAIT MUCH LONGER FOR THE ARRIVAL OF YOUR MAN. PLEASE ADVISE WHEN YOU CAN SEND ANOTHER AGENT. URGENCY IN ALL MATTERS DISCUSSED.

FORBIN

"Damn it all, where are they!"

Wagner looked up to see the boy gaping at him. "Run back to the Western Union office and wait there until it closes."

"But I'm supposed to be off work in another ten minutes," the lad offered. "And the office closes in two hours."

"I'll pay you double," Wagner replied.

Without another word, the boy was off and running.

Wagner realized after he had done it that he could have enlisted one of the other messengers at the going rate, but he didn't let the extravangant expenditure linger in his thoughts.

Again, he sat down at his desk and began to read a rather disturbing letter that concerned the methods used by several of his agents who had tracked down an unsavory robber of riverboats along the Missouri. It happened that the outlaw was popular in the territory, enjoying a reputation as a sort of Robin Hood. He was stealing supplies from the cargo-laden riverboats and giving them to down-and-out settlers who were having trouble making a living from poor farmland.

When the agents apprehended the thief, they were unable to capture him alive and had, in the process of the chase, burned down the outlaw's house. The letter was from the criminal's maiden aunt who was now living on a poor farm due to her nephew's loss of estate. Wagner read the agents' report after he finished the old woman's letter. Indeed, their fugitive had given them little chance to take him alive. And, according to the report, the fire was started by the perpetrator himself.

Wagner dropped both documents on his desk. He took off his spectacles and rubbed his eyes. There was no way for the agency to win in its pursuit of criminals. Someone would always complain, no matter what his agents did. Best just to forget about it and think of . . . of what?

He read the telegram from Forbin again, wondering if the assistant state attorney had made a mistake coming to the agency for help. Forbin seemed desperate enough to enlist some of the officials from his own domain. And yet, if the conspiracy went into the very veins of the inner government, outside help was the only answer.

"Damn it all!"

"William!"

Wagner looked up to see Pinkerton standing in the doorway of his office. "You know I don't tolerate foul language, William."

Wagner held out the telegram. "Sorry. But read this before you judge me too harshly."

After Pinkerton had read the message, he said, "Damn it all."

"What are we going to do?"

Pinkerton groused for a few moments, but then replied, "Wire him back that we can't help him unless he's willing to take the man we assign to the job. Tell him he just has to wait if he wants our help. This thing sounded pretty far-fetched to begin with."

Wagner nodded, adding, "But if it's not?"

Pinkerton exhaled. "That's not our concern. We must send Raider on this. If we send in more than one man, they'll be too visible. If this conspiracy is real, then the conspirators could lay low while our boys are in the area. Raider might be able to slip in among them and ferret out the cause of the problem."

"Raider's more a buffalo than a ferret."

Pinkerton raised an eyebrow. "Well, he has his methods. I'm sure that big galoot is capable of discretion when he wants to be."

Wagner put on his glasses, and looked down at his desk. "I'm just anxious about him and Stokes. One of them should have sent a message by now."

"Nevertheless, we can't pluck them from the earth and drop them where they're needed, William. We don't have the powers of the gods."

Wagner glanced up at his superior. "Should I send the message today?"

Pinkerton suddenly had a strange gleam in his eye. "No. Wait until tomorrow. Mr. Forbin can wait one more day."

"I hope so."

Pinkerton went back into his office.

Wagner started to work again. He was in the middle of a report when the door opened and the messenger boy came running in from the cold street. He was yelling and waving a piece of paper.

"It's here, Mr. Wagner!"

The commotion caused Pinkerton to come out of his office.

Wagner read the telegram and nodded to his boss. "Stokes found Raider."

"And?"

"The big man is on his way to Texas," Wagner replied.

Pinkerton just nodded and turned back into his office, as if he had known all along that things would come out in his favor.

Wagner dismissed the messenger and returned to his papers again, smiling and whistling as he began to work.

CHAPTER NINE

Getting to Austin was a chore. Raider left Stokes and rode south to Kenton, Oklahoma, where he sold the exhausted gray and waited for the stagecoach. The only trouble was, he found out the stagecoach had broken down *after* he sold the gray. When he returned to the livery to buy the horse back, the smithy was asking double what he had paid Raider. Raider had not gotten his back pay, so he was unable to meet the man's price.

So Raider had been lucky enough to hitch a ride on a tinker's wagon, all the way to Texas. He remembered the lies he had heard about tinkers, most of which turned out to be true. Tinkers didn't bathe much, they usually swore a lot more than most men, and if they owed you money, they'd try to chisel you by offering to work it off instead of repaying you. Still, it beat walking or paying for another overpriced horse.

The tinker dropped him in Hartley, Texas, where he finally found a stage company that was running to Amarillo. He could get a train in Amarillo. Raider didn't like riding trains, but the message had said to get to Austin as quickly as possible. Raider liked the urgent sound of the communiqué. Most of his cases had been simple manhunts for the past few months. He was ready to tackle something with a little more intrigue. As good as he was with his fists and his guns, the big man had to admit that he liked the idea of figuring something out, even if it seemed impossible at first.

From Hartley, he set out on the stage, only to be reminded of how much he hated riding in a Concord coach. Then the bridge was down in Dumas, so they had to ride west to ford a river that was swollen with the November rain and snow. Naturally the coach got mired in the river bottom and Raider was elected to help push it out. Then they hit a rocky, chuck-hole road that made the river seem like a hot bath.

Raider bounced into Amarillo, tired and aching, dragging his saddle to the train just as it was getting ready to pull out. He had barely had time to send a cable north to notify the Chicago office of his whereabouts and to ask for his back pay to be wired to Austin. Somehow he managed to board the train without losing anything.

As he leaned back in his seat, he tried to close his eyes, thinking that his troubles were over. He couldn't have been more wrong. The day car was cold and smelly. Several of the windows were broken, which allowed the smoke and soot to seep in, choking the big man awake.

Then, in Lampasas, four toughs got on, whooping and hollering like a bunch of drunk miners. They were just cowboys, carrying their saddles and cursing too much. One by one they eyed Raider, but when he didn't say anything, they kept on with their loudness. Raider watched them carefully, suspecting some sort of robbery attempt.

However, the cowboys only disturbed his sleep. And when one of them got too friendly with a plain young woman who was not interested, Raider was forced to intercede and back him down. The cowboy got tame really fast when he saw the Colt on Raider's hip. His companions were also quick to recognize a man who could handle a gun. Nobody wanted to die unnecessarily, not even a frisky cowpoke.

He tried to get back to sleep after the ruckus, but the cold and the rocking motion kept him half-awake and nauseous all the way into Austin.

When he finally arrived at the entrance to Clay Forbin's office, the big man from Arkansas was exhausted, unbathed, unshaven, and in a thoroughly abominable mood. He pushed through the stately halls of Texas justice with everyone gaping at his unkempt figure. But Raider didn't care what they thought of him. He only meant to carry out his boss's orders, to find Forbin as soon as possible.

The office door was open so Raider pushed in.

Forbin shrieked when he saw him, cowering back against the wall. "No!" he cried. "Please. Did Starbin send you? Please, don't hurt me."

Raider's eyes narrowed. "Are you Forbin?"

"No, I'm not. Please, just go away."

Raider dropped his gear on the floor. He stood there holding his Winchester. Forbin repeated his desire not to be shot.

"I ain't gonna shoot you," the big man said. "I'm Raider. From the Pinkerton Agency. You still need me t' work for you?"

Forbin slowly regained his composure. He came off the wall, wiping his forehead. Raider removed his dusty Stetson, waiting for the nervous man to stop shaking. What the hell was Forbin scared of?

He studied Forbin's pale face. The man had been worrying too much. His lips were sort of bluish and his hands trembled like jelly.

"I'm so glad you made it, Mr. Raider."

"Just Raider."

Forbin hurried around the big man and closed the door. "Raider, this is not a good time. I can't explain it all right now, but you can't stay here. You've already attracted enough attention by coming here directly."

"That's what I was s'posed t' do," the big man said. "Now, d' you need my work or not?"

"I need your assistance, sir. I explained it all to Allan Pinkerton and William Wagner. Didn't they tell you why I wanted you here?"

Raider shook his head. "No. I was just told t' find you quick as I could. Sorry if I was a little late."

Forbin gave him the once-over. "My God, you're about the biggest man I've ever seen."

"Is there somethin' on your mind, Mr. Forbin?"

The assistant state attorney frowned at him. "There's plenty on my mind, sir."

"Why did you jump so high when I showed up? And who's Starbin?"

"I can't talk now, Raider. I . . . shh, what's that?"

Raider turned toward the door. He thought he heard scuffling feet outside, but when he opened the door to look into the hall, there was nobody there. He closed the door and glared at the sweating politician.

"I don't like cat-and-mouse, Forbin. Maybe you oughta just up an' tell me what's goin' on here."

Forbin quickly scrawled something on a piece of paper. "Here, this is my address. Go get yourself cleaned up and meet me tonight at seven o'clock, at my home."

"You sure it can wait?"

"I don't have any of the evidence here," Forbin replied. "Everything is in my private den, locked up safely. Just come at seven."

Raider eyed him, wondering if he should stay. "You sure you're not in some kind a trouble, Forbin? I mean, I was sent here t' help out. Mebbe I oughta stay here."

"Please," Forbin entreated. "You must go. It will be much worse if you remain with me. I'll explain it all tonight."

Raider figured he had to do what he was told, since Forbin and the great state of Texas were paying his wages. He hoisted the saddle on his shoulder and headed back out into the streets of Austin. The rest of the day was spent getting clean. He checked into a hotel where he soaked for an hour in a hot tub. After that, he bought a fresh cotton shirt and a new pair of denims. A shoemaker shined his boots and oiled his vest. By then he was out of money so he called for his back pay at the Western Union.

Wagner had come through with the money. Raider was feeling pretty good by then so he went back to the hotel for a big meal. A bed was next, or so he thought until he realized something important: his hat was looking pretty ragged.

Now a man in a ragged hat could call on a state attorney once, but he had better not go back looking like he had crawled out of a coal yard. Still, buying a hat wasn't an easy task. After all, you had to find the one that fit perfectly, the one with the low brim that let you look at an outlaw without him seeing your eyes.

It took him another hour to find the right hat, so it was late afternoon when his head hit the pillow. He had left word with the clerk to wake him at six-thirty, but somehow things were fouled up and the big man did not awaken on his own until seven. Scrambling to his feet, he dressed in the dark, hurrying to get to his appointment. Forbin was going to think he was a slacker, the kind of man who did things halfway.

When he came out of the hotel, Raider was surprised to find a carriage-for-hire waiting in the street. He flagged the driver and gave him the address of Forbin's home. In a few minutes, he was standing on the front steps, knocking at the door.

But no one answered. Had Forbin gotten tired of waiting and left? Raider tried the door. The door swung open as soon as he touched the knob.

"Forbin?"

He stuck his head in, dropping his hand toward his sidearm.

"It's me, Raider. The Pinkerton."

But the place was dark.

Cautiously, the big man started through the house, watching the shadows.

He stopped still when he heard movement. It seemed to be coming from the back of the house. He drew his Colt and headed toward the thumping sounds that seemed to be growing louder.

A door creaked at the end of a long hallway.

Raider froze with the Colt in front of him. "Forbin?"

More thumping. Scuffling of feet. A raspy noise sounded like somebody gargling. Then a door opened wider and light streaked into the hallway.

Raider thumbed back the hammer of the Colt. "Show yourself, honcho. Come on, slow-like."

A man seemed to slump through the threshold. Raider tensed until he saw that the man was Forbin. His pale face reflected the light from the study where he had been working.

"Damn it," the big man said, holstering the sidearm. "You scared the daylights outta me, Forbin."

No reply from the attorney. He clumped out into the hall, taking slow, deliberate steps. He seemed to be drunk, staggering toward Raider.

"Hey, boy, you okay?"

Raider stepped to meet him.

Forbin coughed and stretched his arms out to the big man. "Starbin," he said. "It was . . ."

Raider caught the man as he fell forward. A Bowie knife was sticking out of Forbin's back. Raider removed the blade, trying to stop the blood that gushed from the deep hole.

"Easy, boy," he said, lowering Forbin to the floor. "Who's Starbin?" he asked. "Come on, tell me."

Forbin's mouth opened but the words never came out. A bubble of blood formed on his lips and then popped as his last breath rushed from his body. Raider knew he had to go for help. But as he stood up, he heard the rifle levers chortling. There were two men drawing a bead on him. And one of them told the big man not to move or he would shot.

Raider kept his hands raised toward the ceiling. He regarded the men who were dressed like Texas Rangers. One of them bent over the body of Clay Forbin and announced that the assistant state attorney was dead. Then he looked at Raider.

"This one done it," he said to his partner.

Raider scowled at the man. "Whoa, honcho. I didn't kill nobody. Forbin there was stabbed when I got here."

The other rifleman nodded to the man who had leveled the accusation. "Yeah, he done it all right."

"Look here, boys, we can straighten this all out if you'll just listen t' me . . ."

Both men gestured with their rifles. One of them said, "Come on, shitbird. We got you dead to rights. Leanin' over the body with the knife in your hand. You killed Forbin and that's all there is to it."

Raider shook his head, trying to smile. "That ain't it at all, pardner. I come t' see Forbin on bus'ness. When I got here he come down this hallway with a knife in his back."

"Save your breath, cowboy. You're just gonna do as you're told if you want to live a while longer. If not . . ."

Of course, Raider had never been one for doing as he was told.

". . . we'll have to plug you. Now, ease that hogleg out of the holster with your left hand . . ."

Raider's black eyes calculated the distances. The rifles were close, which made them hard to wield in the confines of the hallway. A Winchester was great for long shots, but in tight quarters a rifle had its disadvantages, especially if a big Arkansas razorback was moving a little too quick.

When he brought the Colt out of his holster with his left hand, he hesitated, like he was going to try something. Both riflemen snapped to attention. That was when he threw the gun at them, a move that they were not expecting. The heavy pistol struck the man on the right, prompting the other one to let off a burst from his repeater.

But by the time the rifle went off, Raider had ducked low, charging with his shoulder. He caught the shooter in the gut, buffeting him to the floor. Again the rifle went off but the slug caught the ceiling instead of Raider's chest. The big man kept on going for the front door like a bull after the cape of the matador.

"Get him."

"Where is he?"

"Too much smoke."

They both fired again but they missed. Their aim was thrown off by the confusion of smoke and noise. Raider crashed through the front door, tumbling down the steps into the street.

He stopped long enough to reach for the hunting knife in his boot. He also had a derringer in his back pocket. Would two small weapons be enough against a pair of rifles?

Best not to think about it.

Raider started running in the darkness, searching for a place to hide. He wondered if he should have bolted in the first place. If the men were Rangers they might listen to reason. Something about them told him that he was in deep shit. Everything had been too quick, like a setup.

No matter. He had to become scarce. Slipping into an alley between two houses, he stopped and listened to the night. Forbin's neighbors were stirring, no doubt awakened by the gunshots. Austin was becoming a peaceable little town which meant that its citizens were not used to such a ruckus.

He heard the men come out of the house. They stopped to tell the neighbors that everything was under control. They didn't say they were Rangers.

How the hell did they get to Forbin's place so fast?

Somebody had manipulated the whole thing.

He heard the men coming toward him.

Raider slid against a wall, feeling a drain pipe against his back. He considered climbing. He might be safe high up.

What a damned awful mess. He hadn't been in Austin a whole day yet and he was already a fugitive from the law. If they were the law.

"You see him?" called one of the riflemen.

"No. Here, tracks!"

Raider decided to climb the drain pipe. He was scurrying up to the roof of a house when the men saw him. They peppered the wall around him with lead, splintering the clapboard as the big man rolled over onto the roof.

"Son of a bitch, I missed him."

"I missed him too. There, he's running."

They fired again as Raider balanced on the crest of the roof. He ran for the opposite side of the house, hoping there was a way down. More slugs urged him along. They weren't very good shots for Rangers, he thought.

The next house was butted up against the one he had been running across. Raider leaped to the adjacent roof, falling when he hit. He grabbed a chimney to keep himself from tumbling to the ground.

Below him, his pursuers were gaping up into the darkness.

"Where'd he go?"

"He's awful fast."

"Pinkertons are good."

Raider stiffened. He hadn't told them he was a Pinkerton. It *was* a setup after all. But who? Raider hadn't even had time to question Forbin about the reason he had been called to Texas.

"There he is. On the other roof."

"Get him."

They started firing again. Raider let go of the chimney and rolled down the slope of the roof, hoping the fall wouldn't break him. He managed to catch the edge of the rain gutter, hanging there for a few seconds before he let go. The ground was soft when he hit.

The riflemen were coming down the alley after him.

Raider broke into a run, heading for a group of dark buildings behind the houses. He had to lay in wait, to get off a lucky shot with the derringer. Maybe he could drop down with the hunting knife, use a few Indian tricks.

They must have seen him running away because the rifles barked again.

Damn, who were they to keep shooting? Didn't they care if they hit any innocent citizens? Maybe they knew the neighborhood. Maybe it was all part of their plan.

"Did you get him?"

"I don't know. He ran into that stable."

"All right. Slow. But don't let him get away."

"You think I want to let him get away?"

Raider could still hear them as he entered the stable. The smell told him horses were there. A chance to run again. If there was a back door.

He paused in the shadows, waiting for his assailants to enter.

They hadn't counted on him running so there was good reason to believe that they were the only two involved in capturing him. No backup, otherwise men would have been stationed all over the place.

Raider had to get away. Or did he? Running might save his neck but it wasn't going to get the job done. The man he had been sent to help was dead and Raider was seized by a sudden curiosity to know why. After all, he had wished for a case with some intrigue. He had certainly gotten it.

But first he had to take care of the men who were chasing him. Not a good idea to kill them. What if they really were Texas Rangers? He could see the report on Wagner's desk: "Pinkerton murders two lawmen." They'd hang him just as high as any outlaw.

So, if he wasn't going to run, he had to make it look like he had. But how? He moved down the line of horse stalls, causing a commotion among the animals. Movement outside. The riflemen were getting closer.

"Whoozat?"

Raider heard the voice from the loft. He looked up to see a young black man staring down at him. The stable boy had been sleeping above.

Raider climbed the ladder to the loft, holding out his hand to the frightened lad. "What's your name, son?" he whispered.

"Toby, but I . . ."

"Shh. Look here, Toby, there's two bastards with rifles gonna kill us both. And they'll be here any second."

Toby swallowed hard and began to shake. "I don't want to die, mister. I don't want nobody to kill me."

"Shh. Nobody will if you do like I say. Is there a back entrance on this stable?"

"A what?"

"A back door."

Toby nodded. "Yes, sir. I knows just where it is too."

"Good man. Now, you gotta show me the fastest horse in this barn. Come on, let's git down."

"But dem men gonna come in here and shoot us."

"They will if we don't move. Let's go, Toby. Before it's too late."

That prompted the lad to scurry down the ladder with Raider right behind him. There was no time to saddle or bridle the horse. Raider put his hat and vest on the young man and lifted him onto the horse's back. He hoped the boy was quick enough to avoid the inevitable rifle shots that came his way.

"Just hold on to the mane, son. Go as fast as you can an' don't look back. Stay low on the horse's neck an' you'll be fine."

"I'm ascared, mister."

Raider reached into his pocket for a silver dollar. "Here, just hold tight to this. An' if anybody catches you, tell 'em you stopped this horse from runnin' away after a bunch of men came and messed up your stable."

"Yes, sir."

Raider threw open the stable door and slapped the horse on the hindquarters. The animal charged through the opening and headed down the alley as fast as it could run. Raider dove back into a stall just as the two riflemen ran into the stable.

"Damn! There he goes."

"I'm gonna shoot . . ."

Raider held his breath, praying for the boy.

"No! He's gone."

"Are we gonna go after him?"

"Not now. We got to go back and clean up the mess. Damn, he would have to be a Pinkerton."

Another rifle lever spoke in the darkness. The landlord of the house and stable asked what the hell was going on. The two men explained that they were chasing a murderer, a fugitive. The man had killed Clay Forbin, the landlord's neighbor. He had stolen a horse as well.

Raider held his breath, wondering if the landlord was going to call for the stable boy. If they discovered Toby was absent, the two riflemen might figure out what had happened. They might poke around in the stalls until they found Raider lying in the muck. But the landlord was the kind of man who thought of himself first, so he neglected to call out to his attendant. He only bemoaned the loss of his animal as he closed the stable door.

After a few minutes, everything was quiet again. Raider lifted himself out of the stall, thinking that he smelled as bad as the horses. But it didn't matter. He had to get back to Forbin's house. He would watch from the shadows until the riflemen were gone. Then he planned to poke around and answer a lot of questions that were running through his mind.

CHAPTER TEN

Raider hid in the shadows behind Forbin's house, watching as the two riflemen loaded the body into the back of a buckboard wagon. The big man wondered if the newspaper would be full of the killing the next day. Nothing made news like a murder, especially when the alleged killer was a Pinkerton agent. It hadn't taken him long to fall straight into the boiling pot. So much for doing his duty.

The wagon pulled out with both men on the wooden seat. Raider had expected one of them to stay behind, but they didn't seem to think he would return to the house. As far as they knew, the big man was long gone on the stolen horse. Now he had to get into the house without being seen by some rubbernecking neighbor.

He filled his lungs and moved swiftly out of the shadows, heading straight for the front door.

The riflemen hadn't even bothered to lock up. Raider slid through the darkness, heading for the room where Forbin had been working, the room where the knife had been stuck in his back. There was a lot to do. First he had to figure out what Forbin had been working on, why he had been killed. Then he had to contact Wagner and plan his next move.

Forbin's den was arranged in a neat, orderly fashion. His desk contained various stacks of paper from his official work in the government. Raider could barely see in the dimness. He had to light the lamp without being seen from the outside, otherwise he would never be able to go through the papers. He closed the heavy drapes on the lone window of the den. Then he found a match and lit a low flame on an oil lamp.

Something told him that the papers he wanted would not be on the desktop. So he dug deeply into the desk drawers until he came upon a sheaf of papers that had been tied together inside a brown wrapper. The package was labeled, "The East Texas Situation." Below the title was written, "Compiled by Horace Wilbur." The word "deceased" had been scrawled below the man's name. And on the side of the brown package, Forbin or someone had penned, "For the Pinkerton."

Raider unfolded the package and in the dim light of the lamp, he began to read.

The big man could not believe the evidence he had before him. No wonder Forbin had been killed. And the men with rifles might very well have been Rangers. After all, Forbin suspected that the conspiracy reached far into the main channels of the Texas government. But how far? According to the report only Forbin and the governor knew about the conspiracy. And the only other man who had known had been killed after he delivered his report to Forbin.

Raider's thoughts were racing as he tried to map out a strategy. First, he had to contact the agency and tell them what he was onto. Wagner probably already knew about the conspiracy, which meant that Raider had been sent into the mouth of the cougar with little warning about what he was facing. With Wagner behind him, it would be easier for Raider to get to the governor. After all, he had to convince someone that he had not killed Forbin. Otherwise he would have to keep operating as an outlaw.

It was going to be tricky though. He had fled after the two riflemen accosted him. That wouldn't look too good when he started to tell his story. Still, the governor had to believe him, especially if he wanted Raider to get to the bottom of things.

The big man was folding up the papers when he heard the front door open and close.

Somebody stepped slowly through the house, heading for the hallway that led to Forbin's office.

Raider below out the lamp and waited in the darkness.

When the door to Forbin's study swung open, Raider grabbed the man and wrestled him to the floor. He put the derringer to the man's head, telling him to lie still if he wanted to live. He could feel the intruder shaking beneath his weight.

"Please, don't kill me! Take whatever you want, but don't kill me!"

Raider kept the derringer on the man's temple. "I ain't here to take nothin', mister. I'm here to clear up the murder of Clay Forbin, among other things."

The man held his breath and then said, "Are you the Pinkerton sent for by Mr. Forbin?"

"How'd you know that?"

The man's voice seemed to change, becoming more hopeful. "I'm Clay Forbin's assistant, Peter Holt. Are you telling me that Mr. Forbin was killed? I was supposed to meet him here tonight, to discuss this thing with you and him."

Raider wasn't buying it. "I didn't see you with Forbin this afternoon. Where were you?"

"At the law library," the man replied. "Please, let me up. I'll tell you everything."

" 'Bout what?"

"About the situation in east Texas!"

Raider figured Holt might be telling the truth. But he frisked him before he took the derringer away from his temple. No guns on him. Raider eased off and let the man regain his feet.

"What are you doing here, Holt?"

"I told you, Mr. Forbin asked me to meet him at nine o'clock. He said you would be here. And now you're saying he was killed?"

Raider nodded. "Staggered down the hall with a knife in 'is back. Then there were two boys on me like stink on a skunk. Tryin' t' say I killed 'im. They took the body away."

"My God. My God." His voice seemed to sink.

Raider relit the lamp, regarding the dapper figure of Peter Holt. He wore a black suit and a string tie. New Stetson, shined shoes. A regular dandy, the kind of man who would work in the government. Holt was younger than Forbin. He had a handsome, unscarred, unlined face. Dark curly hair and clear brown eyes.

"You say you knew about the thing in east Texas?" Raider asked.

Holt nodded. "Mr. Forbin only told me this week."

That made sense to the big man, although he was not yet ready to trust Holt. He had a few questions first. About the conspiracy.

"S'pose you tell me what Forbin said about east Texas, Holt."

Holt eyed him cautiously. "Maybe I should be asking what

you know. After all, how can I be sure you're the Pinkerton?"

"You cain't. My credentials are back at my hotel. But if you wanna set your mind at ease, I was at Forbin's office just t'day. Caused a big commotion at the justice building."

Holt nodded. "All right, fair enough. I heard about that. But let me ask you this. Does the name Tanner Starbin mean anything to you?"

Raider nodded. "Accordin' t' your late boss, Starbin is the one b'hind the east Texas deal. Or at least that's where the evidence points."

Holt frowned, sighing. "I couldn't believe it either. It all sounded too crazy until Mr. Forbin let me see the documents."

Raider held up the sheaf of papers. His trust for Holt was growing. "Somebody in east Texas seems t' be buildin' an army. The pattern of the robberies was really convincin'. That armory in Dallas was hit pretty hard. At night, too, when nobody would have thought it. Stolen guns, cannons, mortars. All disappeared without a trace."

Holt looked at him straight on. "Mr. Forbin figured there was a railroad connection to the south. Private boxcars supposedly loaded with bricks and iron for building."

"Is that where Starbin comes in?"

Holt nodded. "He does own a couple of rail cars and a single line of track leading into Zavalla."

"Where the hell is that?" Raider asked.

"On the edge of the swampland, north of Beaumont. Starbin has a home there, more like an estate. He controls most of the land in that area. Made all his money growing cotton. He's a former Confederate colonel who made good after the war. But he never has forgiven the north for defeating the south."

"You think that has somethin' t' do with all this?"

Holt shrugged. "Who can say? We're not even sure he's behind any of the robberies."

Raider gestured to the report. "Says here that he has a rail line runnin' from Beaumont to the north."

Holt nodded. "That's another thing. Did you read about the steamers that were hijacked?"

"Stolen gunpowder and lead," Raider replied. "Some dynamite too."

"And the men?"

Raider exhaled. "Yeah, that was the most convincin' part. Says that Starbin claims to be hirin' farmers an' cotton pickers t' work his land. Only most o' the men have reputations. An' a lotta them are former rebels, men who never were able catch on t' real work after the war."

"Starbin's own regiment seems to be gathering down there," Holt rejoined. "Wilbur counted nearly fifty men. Said they were all stashed out in the swampland along with the stolen goods."

Raider wiped the sweat from his brow. "Damn. How can this Starbin hide a hundred tons of hardware in a swamp? Unless . . ."

"Go on."

"Barges," Raider replied. "Shallow water flatboats like the ones they use in Louisiana. He could off-load the cargo onto wagons an' then transfer it from rail t' boat. It would take a long time, but accordin' t' this report, all o' this has been happenin' over the past two years."

"Slow and steady," Holt said.

Raider grunted, throwing the report onto Forbin's desk. "Your boss was smart t' figger all this. His main lead was that armory job in Dallas. He knew he was in danger too."

Holt frowned again. "How do you figure that?"

"He didn't want me hangin' 'round the justice buildin'," Raider replied. "An' he told you 'bout ever'thin'. He wanted somebody else t' know what was goin' on in case anythin' happened to 'im."

"Makes sense. But what are we going to do now?"

Raider glanced at the dapper gentleman who seemed to be scared as hell. "Well, the first thing is, I gotta clear my name. I gotta get t' the gov'nor somehow and then head for Zavalla. Or Beaumont. Beaumont might be the best place t' begin."

Holt nodded in agreement. "I can square things with the governor. But I wonder if we want to let everyone know that your name is cleared?"

Raider scowled at the politician. "Come agin?"

"If you were known to be the man who killed Forbin, you might infiltrate Starbin's army more easily. He'd appreciate the man who stopped his main adversary. Your reputation would precede you."

Raider thought about it for a while, then said: "Mebbe. But how are you gonna stop the Rangers an' the Austin sheriff from comin' after me? Once the rumors start flyin', every lawman in Texas is gonna be lookin' for my hide. Hell, I won't even be able t' wire my bosses without the clerk tippin' off the local law."

"Leave that to me," Holt replied. "I'm the one you have to trust now. Clay Forbin is gone."

Raider grabbed the front of the man's coat and pulled him up so they were face to face. "I don't trust no one, Holt. But I'm gonna give you a chance. If you come through for me, then I'll work with you."

"What do you want me to do?" the man asked tentatively.

"We're goin' back t' my hotel. Then you're gonna get my gear for me. After that, you're gonna get me a hoss. Then I want you t' write me a letter sayin' that I'm workin' for the gov'nor. In case anyone gets on my tail. You think you can pull that off?"

Holt nodded, even though his expression was dubious. "I think I can."

"Good. Then when I'm on my way, you can square things with the gov'nor an' wire my agency. Tell 'em what's happenin', how I'm workin' with you now 'stead o' Forbin. Got that?"

"Yes."

"And as for the outlaw story . . . that's not a bad angle. If I hit east Texas with a reputation, it might be better, just like you said. Only the real lawmen will have t' know t' leave me alone."

Holt nodded again. "The Rangers won't bother you. And once you're out of Austin, there won't be any wanted posters issued. Although, I don't know how Starbin will hear about you."

"Word o' mouth," the big man replied. "Your late boss figgered that somebody was actin' like a leaky bucket. If that's true, Starbin will know 'bout me a lot quicker'n anybody else."

"Good thinking. We'd better get going."

Raider let him go and then put a finger in his face. "If you cross me, Holt, I'll kill you as dead as your boss."

"Don't worry, I won't."

As they started out of the study, Holt's foot kicked something heavy on the floor. It was Raider's Colt, lying where the two riflemen had left it. The big man picked it up and slipped it into his holster.

"Do you know how to use that thing?" Holt asked.

Raider grimaced at him. "You don't wanna know, ol' buddy. And you sure as hell don't wanna find out the hard way."

Holt was sure he didn't.

They left the house, walking through back alleys until they reached the hotel. Holt went in the back door and did not come out for almost an hour. When he returned, he was carrying all of Raider's gear, including the big man's Winchester.

"Did you see anyone guardin' my room?" Raider asked.

Holt replied that he had seen a man with a rifle in the hall. He had rented the room next to Raider's in order to gain access unseen. It had taken him a long time to move the gear quietly and then to get it out of the room into the stairwell without being noticed.

"Good work, boy. How 'bout that letter?"

Holt gave him a piece of folded parchment. "I wrote it while I was in the room. I had to use a pencil because there wasn't a pen."

"No matter. You done good. Now, we gotta find a hoss."

"I'll give you my own," Holt replied. "It's in the livery up the street. A black stallion. He's rough to handle, but . . ."

"I'll make do. Let's go."

In no time at all, Raider was saddled up and ready for the long trip.

Holt also gave him money, about forty dollars. "It's all I have," the politician said.

"It'll be enough. You just make sure you square things on this end. And make sure you contact my bosses. Let 'em in on what's really happenin'."

"I'll do my best."

Raider swung into the saddle and turned the animal toward the east. "If you don't hear from me in a month, send in somebody t' look for me."

"Send a wire to my home address," Holt rejoined. "It's written on the letter I gave you."

"Thanks."

"Good luck, Raider."

"Sure."

He spurred the black and rode hard away from Austin.

CHAPTER ELEVEN

William Wagner was not really expecting any surprises in the morning mail. It had been a long time since he had heard from Raider, but that was not unusual, given the big man's methods of operation. Nor had he received any word from the office of the state attorney in Texas. So when the large envelope arrived at Fifth Avenue in Chicago, Wagner tore it open, thinking it was something else entirely.

His eyes bulged when he read the newspaper clipping.

Immediately, he rose from his desk and headed for the door of Allan Pinkerton's office.

Pinkerton read the clipping with the same sense of trepidation. "My God, can this be true?"

The headline from the *Austin Weekly Chronicle* read: "Attorney Murdered in Own Home. Pinkerton Agent Suspected."

Pinkerton searched the envelope for some sort of letter, but the clipping was the only enclosure.

"Why is this the first we've heard of it?" he asked.

Wagner shook his head. "I don't know. But Forbin is dead now and Raider is supposed to have been the one who killed him."

"It doesn't make any sense. Surely we would have heard from Raider by now. Why would he kill Forbin and simply disappear?"

Wagner sighed. "I don't know. Maybe this is all some sort of ploy engineered by that big dumb razorback. He could have had the good sense to fill us in. Maybe this clipping is his way of telling us what he's up to. I can't believe he would kill Forbin."

"Nor can I."

Pinkerton looked at the paper which was dated more than

three weeks ago. "I don't think he's in Austin now."

"No, that would make sense. If he's anywhere, he's probably heading east. What was the name of that town where Tanner Starbin lives?"

"Zacalla?" Pinkerton replied. "Zamalla?"

"Just a moment . . ."

Wagner went back to his desk and returned with the correct information. "Zavalla, Texas," he said. "That's where Raider is headed."

Pinkerton shook his head. "I don't like this, William. If Raider is really on the lam, he wouldn't have stayed around in Austin to mail us this newspaper clipping. Maybe he's working with someone we don't know about. After all, Forbin is gone now. Maybe he's in league with somebody from the governor's office."

"Perhaps." Wagner exhaled his frustration. "I'll get off a wire to the governor's office immediately."

"No," Pinkerton said. "That won't do. Remember, Forbin thought the conspiracy went straight into the government. We can't stir up anything now. It's too late anyway. Raider is working the best way he knows how and we don't want to foul him up."

"We have to do something," Wagner pleaded. "I don't want him running around down there with half the state on his tail."

Pinkerton rubbed his beard, thinking. Finally he said, "All right. We'll send another one of our own men. Has Stokes delivered that man to Idaho yet?"

"Yes, but I was going to send him to . . ."

"To Texas," Pinkerton replied. "As soon as possible."

After Wagner thought about it for a moment, he agreed that it was the right thing to do.

CHAPTER TWELVE

Raider rode out of Austin, leaving Holt to patch up the rough spots. He wondered if maybe it had been a bad idea to bolt with so many loose ends, but as Holt had said, he did benefit from a certain status that came with being an assassin. Whether he had killed Forbin or not, the word of the attorney's death would be enough to make his name notorious. He hoped it would help him down the road somewhere when he ran into the man named Tanner Starbin.

As the black stallion loped over the sloping plain, Raider considered the evidence he had found in Forbin's office. Something bad was certainly happening in east Texas, but the big man knew enough about conspiracies to realize that surface evidence wasn't always an indicator of what lay beneath obvious explanations.

Somebody had been stealing munitions and Tanner Starbin did have the inside track as the main suspect. But Forbin's first investigator had filed brief, sketchy reports that might not bear up with the right explanation. After all, it was no sin to keep iron and powder on hand, providing that it hadn't been stolen. Maybe the investigator—what was his name—had seen something he didn't quite understand and had interpreted the facts in the wrong way. Or maybe he hadn't.

Who the hell was Tanner Starbin anyway? Some old Confederate colonel who decided to have a reunion with his former unit. Then again, if that first report was right, a lot of lone guns and hard men had been finding their way to Zavalla. Raider recognized the names of a couple of men he had put away in the territorial prison. They would be real happy to see him.

Which meant a lot of adjustments on the trail.

• • •

First and foremost, he could not go into any large towns on his ride east. He had to take a straight route through the little holes-in-the-wall that were trying to become real towns. Elgin, Giddings, Antry, Lake Coe. Even then he only went into the sun-baked hamlets if he needed something. Otherwise he just circled around, trying to keep out of sight, letting the trail change his appearance.

His beard grew again, the sun baked him, he became dark and crusty from the chalky trail. He wanted to look mean when he got where he was going. He wanted men to step aside when he stomped down a sidewalk. He wanted women to shun him and shield the eyes of their children.

Raider wanted to be the man who shot Clay Forbin, the Pink who had gone bad and was sinking into the mire. If Tanner Starbin was recruiting dirty guns, the big man from Arkansas planned to be the dirtiest. He had to be the kind of gunslinger who could find employment in a private army.

He kept on the trail, eating whatever he could shoot or dig out of the ground. Part of him enjoyed the freedom and the peace of mind. Just the wind and the bluebonnets that began to disappear as he drew closer to the coastal plains of the Texas shore. The ride into Beaumont took about two weeks, he thought. He had decided to start there instead of riding straight into Zavalla. Sometimes you had to take the roundabout path if you were going to get what you wanted.

Raider thought the pecan trees and wooded hammocks of east Texas reminded him a lot of Arkansas, at least in the flatter parts. White-tailed deer were as thick as rabbits and almost as small. He knew he was close to the gulf when he saw seagulls circling over a large, inland lake. Gulls were as bad as buzzards when it came to eating anything dead. Sea vultures that squawked.

If he didn't find what he needed in Beaumont, he might have to head all the way down to Port Arthur. Not much further, really, but he wasn't sure how much time he had to waste. What if there really was a man building an army in east Texas? And what if he had plans to take over the whole damned state?

Nobody could pull it off, Raider thought. How could somebody even think they were going to repel the militia and the U.S. Cavalry? Of course, he had seen madder men with madder notions in his day.

What if somebody really tried to take over the Lone Star state?

Raider hadn't been in Beaumont for quite some time. He didn't remember much about the town and he hadn't really been so close to the Gulf of Mexico since he and his old partner had tangled with a man named Lin Ching. Even then they had been over in Galveston and Texas City.

Still, Beaumont was like any other town. It had a bright side and a dark side. A man could have a high time or a low time. He could laugh or he could bleed. Raider figured it was going to take blood.

Slipping unseen into the bustling settlement required a night ride. He had to circle back and come in from the east. He chose a livery in the seedy section, a place where he would not have left the stallion if the occasion hadn't called for it. Everything had to be smooth, subtle. Raider hoped to be found and in the process find what he was looking for.

Next came the flophouse, the kind of sleeping establishment where you kept your hand on your gun. Allan Pinkerton and William Wagner wouldn't have let their least favorite house pet sleep in such a place. It had no name and it smelled of unwashed men who drank too much.

But Raider just let his face hit the pillow and he slept there with his hand on his Colt.

The next morning, he woke and headed back to the livery. He hung around there all day, talking to the black man who was beating iron into horseshoes. Not really pungent conversation, just grunts and groans, a few lies told and agreed with.

Toward dusk, the smithy asked him if he was going to talk all night.

Raider said he would settle for a cheap whore and a bottle of homemade whiskey. The smithy told him to try the Mexican section. Then he gave the big man directions.

Walking with his shoulders bent, Raider took the back alleys, trying to be seen and not seen at the same time. Not seen by lawmen, seen by the men he needed to find. Men who would lead him eventually to Tanner Starbin or whoever was causing all the ruckus in east Texas.

But what ruckus? Nothing had really happened. Then why did he feel like something was happening? For the first time since he had taken the case, Raider felt his instincts starting to work. His breath quickened and his heart beat faster. He was on the trail of something he had to figure out. Even if it seemed unfigurable.

But nothing happened the first night. They eyed him in the Mexican section as he drank tequila and fondled a fat whore. They watched him leave with her, although they did not see him pay her outside to get rid of her. He planned to stay away from women for a while, at least until he had made some progress.

But nobody approached him that night, so it was back to the flophouse for another night of fitful sleep. Raider had to kill a few bugs that bit him awake. And some time during the night he had to slug a man who was trying to steal his gear. The next morning, he couldn't remember if he had dreamed hitting the would-be thief smack in the face.

The second day saw the big man at the corrals on the edge of town. Beef was starting to be shipped through Beaumont to New Orleans and Baton Rouge. Corn, wheat, and cotton also moved through on rail cars to Port Arthur. Trains and cattle brought the rough kind of men needed to do such work. Raider found his share of toughs in Beaumont.

When he approached a group of idlers at the corral, they sized him up, acting like it didn't matter that this tall ape had blown in. Just another saddle tramp looking for day wages. Only Raider didn't talk about day wages. He mimicked other sorry men he had heard in his travels, bemoaning the trap of honest work, wishing aloud that there was some way for a poor man to make a buck without breaking his back.

None of this idle talk brought results, however. Nobody knew of any work for a dumb man except the kind that breaks the back. Still, one or two agreed that a man had to take chances to get rich and one pair of dark eyes glistened when Raider pulled back his coat to reveal the butt of the Colt on his hip. The sheriff came along to break up the gathering after a while, but by then Raider was back at the blacksmith's shop.

He brought whiskey, hoping the smithy would talk. "You want a drink there, Jasper?"

"Name ain't Jasper," the black man replied. "And I don't take no drink. I has to preach on Sunday and I can't be full of liquor if I'm gonna take my flock to heaven."

Raider nodded. "Can't disagree with that."

The black man turned hateful eyes on him. "You can't, huh? When's the last time you's in church, cowboy?"

"I ain't sure I ever been in one," Raider replied, playing along.

The smithy shook his head. "Forgive him, Jesus."

"Look here, preacher. I was wonderin' if you could tell me a few things. I'm lookin' for somebody."

The smithy slammed the hammer against hot iron. "Git on away from me, cowboy. I doan feel like jawwin' no more tonight."

"Hey, you don't have t' . . ."

"That's right, chalky, I don't have to do nothin'. I know my skin is colored and I got to work down here wid choo white trash, but I doan have to take no sass and I doan have to associate wid choo."

Raider felt sort of bad inside. But that was what it had come to. He had let himself sink so low that good, Godfearing commonfolk wouldn't even talk to him anymore. That saddened him in a strange way, like somebody seeing a situation from the other side. He was doing his job too well.

"Sorry, smithy, I . . ."

The man waved the hammer at him. "Just git gone, boy, before I have to pound you into the ground."

Raider slinked away, feeling like the most miserable shitheel who had ever drawn breath. But hell, he really couldn't blame the smithy for shunning him. Given a choice, he wouldn't have kept company with himself either.

That night, things seemed to come alive in the Mexican section. It was Saturday evening, which meant that every cowboy with a dollar and a hard dick had come into town. They knew where to congregate in those dark places the law tended to overlook. They drank and gambled and fought over whores who cared nothing about them.

Raider went in among them, keeping his eyes open, trying to look suspicious and guilty. He was the rabid wolf in search of the lair, the impatient man-eating cougar with a hunting party on his trail. He picked the worst-smelling cantina to ply his trade.

He wondered what it would take to trigger the kind of thing he needed. It had to be quick and brutal. Or at least brutal.

The kind of fight he was looking for had to be remembered.

He tried everything. Making comments about ugly whores and the men whose laps they were sitting on. Nothing beyond the men backing down. Then he tried to get into it with a fat man, insisting that the bottle of tequila on the man's table belonged to him. But the man only gave up the bottle.

What the hell was wrong? Most people in Texas would fight over anything. Raider tried to besmirch the glorious name of the great Alamo state, but nobody seemed to care. He *had* sunk pretty far.

When he reached the end of his patience, he turned and started out of the cantina, planning to try another establishment.

Only then did it happen, and in the craziest way.

Raider did little more than throw a glance in the direction of a muscular, scar-faced cowboy. Their eyes locked for a second and then Raider turned for the door. The rocky voice called him back.

"What the hell are you lookin' at, peckerwood?"

Raider hesitated, wheeling back to see if anyone had a gun in hand. No iron flashing in the torchlight of the cantina. The cowboy had the hawk-stare leveled on him. The spectators were silent, anticipating the outcome.

"You talkin' t' me, gopher-dick?"

That was a good one. *Gopher-dick.* Raider had come up with it on the spur of the moment. Just slipped out. Perfect.

The evil-eyed cowboy tensed. He stood up from his chair. As tall as Raider, big fists and arms. It wouldn't be a short fight.

"How you want it?" Raider asked. "Guns or knives?"

"You chicken to try your fists?" the cowboy challenged.

Oohs and ahs from the crowd. Bets went down. Everybody jockeyed for a better view of the fracas.

"Fists are fine with me," Raider replied. "But I'll shoot any man that comes between us."

"Outside," the cowboy said. "I been lookin' for a fight for two weeks."

Raider grinned, glad that it had finally begun. "Well, asshole, it looks like you found one."

As soon as they were outside, the rough-faced cowboy tried to sneak around the side with a sucker punch to Raider's jaw.

Luckily the big man saw it coming out of the corner of his eye. He managed to duck out of the way so the cowboy's fist caught the air, making him lurch off balance. Raider used the opportunity to lay his best haymaker upside the cowboy's head.

What happened next startled the tall Pinkerton from Arkansas. He expected the cowboy to go down, but instead the man only shook his head and smiled. Raider felt the stinging in his knuckles. His instincts had been right before; it wasn't going to be a short fight.

"Damn," the cowboy said. "That the best you got?"

More bets went down.

Raider raised his fists again, hoping he could find a way to hurt the scarred drifter. "At least I wasn't tryin' t' bushwhack you."

The cowboy came on again, throwing wild rights and lefts. Raider caught most of the blows on his arms, but they were still hard enough to make it sting wherever they landed. Even though the cowboy was strong, Raider hoped he would eventually punch himself out.

Faces in the crowd began to slack when they saw that the cowboy couldn't take Raider down. The big man flicked his left, counterpunching, landing bee-stingers on the scarred nose of his opponent. Each time the cowboy's head snapped back, a little more fight seemed to go out of him.

Finally he stopped to take a breath. "You slimy bastard," he growled, showing brown teeth. "If you . . ."

Raider didn't wait to see what if. He came with the left, feinting, dropping the overhand right as the cowboy took the fake. His fist crunched the man's mouth, forcing him to spit out two front teeth. Blood poured from his mouth and nose.

The betting got hotter as they all shifted to Raider.

As the cowboy started to circle him, Raider moved too, keeping his feet directly under him for balance.

"Gonna git you," the cowboy lisped through his bloody mouth.

"I'm right here, shit-hook."

Raider felt sort of bad about pounding the old boy. He was just a drunk trail hand looking for a good time on Saturday night. Of course, the fight was all part of that weekend's fun.

The cowboy charged head on. Raider would have dodged him too, if one of the men from the crowd hadn't tripped him.

The big man went down and the cowboy fell on top of him.

Raider knew it was time for payback. The cowboy used his advantage to land several blows on the big man's face. But the punches had no leverage and Raider barely felt them. He managed to get a hand free to grab the cowboy's throat.

Somebody in the crowd cried out, "He's got a knife."

Raider looked up to see the blade glinting in the torchlight. He expected the polished steel to fall, to engorge the soft flesh of his throat. He had to get the other hand free; had to grab the man's wrist.

A pistol exploded, flashing fire in the dim shade of evening.

The knife flew out of the man's hand.

Immediately he jumped off Raider, searching the crowd for the smoking pistol.

Raider was up beside him, ready to do battle again.

"Who shot the knife out of my hand?" the cowboy cried.

The crowd parted and a small, stocky man stepped toward the center of the fracas. "I did."

The cowboy's eyes grew wider and his face slacked. He was obviously afraid of the gunman, but he managed to say gruffly: "You didn't have to do that, Fernandez."

The gunman gestured with the barrel of a shining Peacemaker. "Y'all said no knives or guns back in the bar."

"Yeah, but . . ."

"No buts, boy. The stranger here didn't pull on you. Hell, he's been kickin' your worthless ass all over the place. And if you're gonna fight him, you're gonna do it like you agreed."

Raider glared at the stocky man. He was short but muscular, probably Mexican, although he spoke like a Texan. His face could not be seen clearly beneath the brim of his sombrero.

"I can fight my own battles," Raider offered.

Fernandez gestured with the Colt again. "Have at it."

Raider grinned. He had found the man he wanted. He was sure of it.

But he had to get past the cowboy first.

Again the scar-faced man came up with a sucker punch. This time, however, Raider did not see it coming. The blow caught him on the hard part of the skull, staggering him a little. But he did not go down.

Thinking he had the advantage, the cowboy drove hard

again, throwing wild rights and lefts. Raider ducked into his arms, fending off the crazy punches as best he could while he regained his sensibilities. When the power flowed back into his arms and legs, he decided it was time to end it.

Betting shifted back to the cowboy.

Raider disappointed them. As soon as scar-face had taxed his strength, the big man roared back, hammering the cowboy with strong, well-timed rights and lefts. It was no contest thereafter. Raider turned the tide, reducing the man's nose to a bloody mass. A few more teeth hit the ground as well.

The cowboy reeled, staggering forward, throwing aimless blows at someone who was no longer there.

Raider timed one last haymaker, bringing it up from the ground, landing it squarely on the man's jaw.

When the cowboy fell face first into the dust, those who had bet on him begged him to get up.

The ones who had bet on Raider pressed for their payoffs.

The man named Fernandez stepped up to pronounce the end of it. "He's gone. Stranger here beat him fair and square."

A few men grumbled, but they weren't ready to stand up to the man in the sombrero.

Raider knew he had found his quarry. But he couldn't appear too eager. He had to play it just right. Even if Fernandez wasn't the one exactly, he could probably steer Raider in the right direction.

"Yeah," Fernandez said, "He's long gone."

Raider started away from him. "So am I, pardner."

For a moment, he thought Fernandez was not going to take the bait.

But the man in the sombrero called out to him. "What's your rush, stranger? Ain't you got time for a drink?"

Raider turned halfway, glaring back at him. "If you had just kicked the cock o' the walk, would you stick around?"

Fernandez tipped back his sombrero, smiling. "Man's got a right to be where he wants to be. Free country, ain't it?"

Raider hesitated, like he was thinking about it. "What if that boy an' his buddies sneak 'round an' try t' get off a lucky shot?"

"You look like you can take care of yourself."

Raider shrugged. "Mister, I ain't got a peso t' my name. Fact is, I'm lookin' for a grubstake just now."

Fernandez nodded. "I can see that. You look like you dropped out of the ass end of a buffalo."

"I prob'ly smell like it too."

"Come on, stranger. I'll buy you a bottle and some beans."

Again the big man hesitated. "Cain't cotton t' no charity."

"Don't worry," Fernandez replied. "You won't."

They chose another cantina, a quieter place. Fernandez ordered food and drink, which was brought almost immediately. Raider figured he had a man with some kind of power, at least around Beaumont. Now he had to play the role, the rough-and-tumble outlaw looking to hire on as a gun.

He looked sideways at Fernandez. "You don't talk like no Mexican."

He expected the man to bristle, but Fernandez only smiled. "My daddy was, but I never knew him. My momma was Anglo."

Raider nodded. "Don't take no offense. I ain't got nothin' agin nobody."

"None taken."

Raider dug into his plate of beef and beans, eating the way he had seen cruder men eat, slurping and making noises.

"You sure are hungry," Fernandez said, still smiling.

"Man with a empty belly wants t' fill it."

Fernandez stopped smiling. "Hunger can do odd things to a man, stranger. You got a name?"

"Not yet."

Fernandez nodded. "I hear you. What kind of stake you lookin' for? You a trail hand?"

Raider paused with his mouth full. "I trailed," he muttered. "I hated it. Same way I hated farmin' an' stagecoach drivin'. The way I hate ever friggin' job I ever had."

Fernandez leaned back in his chair. "You ain't leavin' yourself much room, stranger."

"Call me Buck. For now."

"You ain't leavin' yourself much room, Buck."

Raider belched. "Man on the run don't have much room."

"What are you runnin' from?"

Raider figured it was time to let half the ball drop. "Let's jus' say I killed a real important man in Austin."

"The Pinkerton!" Fernandez cried. "You . . ."

Raider was confused by what happened next. There were

shouts and some confusion at the entrance to the cantina. Suddenly Fernandez was on his feet, drawing his Peacemaker. He was damned fast, too.

Twice the Colt barked. Raider thought he was going to be the target, but instead, a dark figure in the doorway fell forward. Raider stood quickly, bringing out his own weapon, slightly behind Fernandez. It was all over, though.

Fernandez holstered his .45. "That stupid damn cowboy," he said. "I reckon he thought he'd sneak back and plug you because you whupped him."

"I better be gittin'," Raider said, sliding his own iron into leather.

Fernandez stopped him. "Hold on, boy, I thought you wanted a grubstake."

Raider smirked at the stocky man. "I ain't cleanin' out your stables," he replied. "I don't care if you did just save my life."

Fernandez laughed. "Boy, you are a hard one. I'm tellin' you, it ain't like that at all. I can find you the kind of work you want."

"Yeah?" the big man replied skeptically. "And what kinda work might that be?"

"Usin' that hogleg you got on your hip," Fernandez offered. "You're fast. Almost as fast as me."

Raider wanted to say he was faster, but he didn't think it was the time to go in that direction. Such arguments could too easily get out of hand. Best just to play along.

"I do owe you," he said to Fernandez.

"Then sit down and let me buy you another drink. Hell, you didn't even finish your dinner."

"I'm willin' t' listen," Raider offered. "As long as it don't cost me nothin'."

"Don't worry, boy. I get it on the other end."

They sat down.

Raider listened as Fernandez described the man in Zavalla, the former Confederate colonel who was looking for fast guns. Paying top wages too. Taking good care of his hands.

Raider asked why Fernandez wasn't up in Zavalla working for the man.

The stocky man shook his head. "I ain't that desperate."

Raider eyed him. "Tell me somethin', Fernandez. You ever meet a man name o' Holt, Peter Holt?"

"Don't ring a bell. But I don't get out of Beaumont much. Only reason I know about this colonel is that he had a boy down here looking for men. I told him I'd keep an eye out. Make sure you tell him I sent you when you get there, Buck."

"What makes you think I'm goin'?" Raider said.

Fernandez laughed. "Hell, boy, where else you got to go?"

The next morning, Raider saddled his horse and rode north toward Zavalla.

CHAPTER THIRTEEN

Raider felt good about the way things had gone in Beaumont. As he drove hard to the north on the stallion, he considered the way his instincts and his deception had been like the twin double barrels of a good Remington shotgun. Of course, it could have been bad, a total miss of the quail on the wing, but since it had worked so well, he decided to give himself a little pat on the back. Nothing big, just an occasional shot from a whiskey bottle that he had purchased at the cantina. He wasn't getting drunk, only taking the edge off the ride.

His second choice for a place to start would have been Port Authur. After all, the hijacked steamers had been hit just off Sea Rim, at the mouth of the harbor. But the long arm of Tanner Starbin also reached south to Beaumont where the tie had been made. Dallas, where the armory had been robbed, was too far north and nowhere near as close to Starbin. And riding straight into Zavalla could have been dangerous, possibly fatal. You didn't play to an adversary's strength, especially when he had an army to back him up.

The big man had been surprised to hear that Fernandez had already heard of the Pinkerton on the run. Holt had done a good job of spreading the word. Maybe too good. What if some local sheriff tried to be a hero and take Raider into custody? As much as the tall Pinkerton disliked the local constabularies, he still wouldn't feel right about killing one in a gunfight.

But he decided to worry about that kind of thing when it came along. Best to focus on the trail. Make a quiet trip north. Avoid strangers and towns. Shoot a few rabbits or quail for dinner. Pull up wild onions and radishes.

He could feel it coming as he got closer to the center of the mystery. No way to skirt around it now. He was riding straight into the gator's mouth. He just hoped the damned reptile didn't have too many teeth.

Almost as soon as he had cleared Beaumont, Raider hit the eastern forests of the Lone Star state. This was a different Texas, away from the arid plains of the west. Here was the Neches River, lined with pine trees and cottonwoods, shaded mud banks that were nothing like the sandy shoals of the Rio Grande. Raider wasn't sure he liked this part of Texas. There were too damned many places to hide, too many spots to disguise an ambush.

He came out of Big Thicket, pushing over the Neches toward Woodville. He remembered a large lake with no name, a friendly shore where he had once pitched a tent and a bedroll.

He wondered if he would be able to send a wire from Woodville. Had news of his notoriety reached that far? He could make the message short and sweet. Sign it with just his initial, let Wagner know he was alive and give them his location. What if he got into Starbin's place and didn't get out? Even if he was killed, somebody should know what was going on and where it was happening.

Maybe it was the little nips of liquor that had him addled, but he decided to go into Woodville to see if it had a wire office. The black covered the ground easily, slowing when it reached the town line. Raider loped the big stallion down the main street, realizing too late that a tall, rough-looking stranger on a black horse would attract a great deal of attention.

Several citizens were glaring at him from the porch of the general store, pointing at the big man from Arkansas and then pointing back at a piece of paper on the wall. Some men were gesturing to the same poster on the front of the livery.

Raider eased his mount up to the stable and squinted at the black-and-white notice that had been tacked onto the livery door.

The wanted poster read: "Five hundred dollar reward for the arrest or capture of *Raider*. Wanted for murder and the theft of a black stallion in Austin." His face blanched white and his stomach leaped off a high cliff. A sketch of his face had been included on the poster.

"That's him!" somebody cried.

Raider spurred the black, racing through town as a few errant shots exploded in the air. He cleared the buildings and turned east, heading for the shores of the lake where he had camped before. Only this time he wasn't going to stop until he reached the north end of the water. The good citizens of Woodville probably wouldn't send out a posse, but there was no reason to take a chance. Where the hell had that poster come from anyway?

Raider figured Holt had something to do with it. Maybe the politician wasn't really on his side. Or maybe somebody else had done it, somebody who got word of Raider's "crimes" in Austin. He had more than a few enemies, men he had sent to prison, men who would love to see *him* at the end of a rope.

When he reached the lake, he turned north along the bank, fighting the black to keep it from drinking. He'd let the stallion water as soon as it had cooled down. The horse would get sick if it drank while it was lathered.

The damned wanted poster.

He turned a bend on the shoreline to come upon three people huddled around a fire. The embers glowed in the early shadows of dusk. Raider was so close that he startled the three campers, a black man and woman with their child.

He reined up and got out of the saddle. "Sorry, folks."

The man laughed. "Lordy, you scared the devil out of me."

The woman glared at him. Her child was crying. "How come you ridin' in on people and scarin' 'em half to death?"

Raider exhaled, shaking his head. "I know that was downright low of me, ma'am, but I do ask your forgiveness."

The woman cradled the crying child in her arms.

"Little girl?" Raider asked.

She nodded.

The man was silent as he stirred the cast iron pot that hung over the fire. Raider suddenly smelled the food. He wondered if the family had enough to share. They looked to be dirt poor.

"Where you hail from, mister?" Raider asked.

The man looked up suspiciously. "Ain't never had no white man call me *mister* before. But I reckon I'm from Mississippi. Headin' to Texarkana to see my wife's kin. Gonna live there, I reckon. Hard times, sir. Hard times."

"It's gonna be better in Texarkana," the wife offered.

The child had fallen asleep in her arms.

Raider stared at the pot which was boiling with deep fat. "Whatchoo fryin' there?"

"Catfish," the man replied. "This lake here is full of 'em. Fryin' some hush puppies too. Used the last of the cornmeal today."

"I'll pay you for a piece of fish and a hush puppy," Raider offered.

The wife shook her head. "We ain't got enough."

Dirt poor, Raider thought. She was only thinking of her kid. Sometimes the world just dealt bad cards to people, mostly honest folks who wouldn't take a nickel they hadn't earned.

The husband waved her off. "Hush up, Lina." Then to Raider, "Don't have but two hush puppies, sir. But I do have more catfish'n we can eat. I can sell you two of them."

Raider reached into his pocket, pulling out the scrip money that Peter Holt had given him. "Forty-one dollars sound all right?"

The man did a double take. "How much?"

"Here, take it, pardner. You need it more'n I do. An' if I have things straight, you're gonna be 'bout the only man in this end o' Texas who ain't gonna be tryin' t' shoot my ass off. Oh, sorry, ma'am."

Raider handed him the money. He also asked him if he wanted the bottle of whiskey. No more nipping on the trail. It may have eased the pain but it made for bad judgments. The man said he didn't drink so Raider poured it out.

After he had eaten his two catfish, Raider asked the man if he had seen anything extraordinary. The man did say that he had seen five or six gunmen riding north from Louisiana, but they didn't speak to him or even try to rob him. He described them as evil men, the kind who looked the other way when they rode by a church or a graveyard.

"They was men like you!" the woman offered, glaring at the big man.

"Hush up, woman," the husband rejoined.

Raider just smiled. "Judge not," he said to her. "Ain't that what the good book says?"

She did not reply.

Raider got on the stallion. "Don't let nobody take that money away from you, honcho."

"No, sir. I won't."

The man waved and Raider dug hard to the north again.

"Forty-one dollars," the wife said. "My sister's gonna be glad to see us now."

The husband stirred the coals of the fire. "I never thought I'd meet a white man I could like," he offered. "He wasn't bad at all."

"No," the woman replied, "but I'll bet he's in trouble."

Even though the people of Woodville did not mount a posse to follow him, Raider still rode through the night. He left the shore of the lake to follow a path through thin forests that teemed with wildlife. All night he heard the squealing of bobcats and night birds. Deer and raccoons were as plentiful as cows on a trail drive. Once he even thought he heard the yowling of a cougar on the prowl. It might have scared him if he hadn't been more afraid of what lay ahead.

Having spent most of his detective days in the western territories, Raider was not completely comfortable in east Texas. He had been through the area several times, but he didn't know it as well as he did the rest of the state. Of course, now was the time to learn. If he didn't catch on in a hurry, they might ship him home in a pine box.

By daybreak he was watching the sun rise over a stand of cypress trees. He had reached the edge of a great swamp. Mosquitoes hovered around him to look for a place to bite. The air was warm even though it was almost December. Somewhere a bigmouth bass popped the top of the water, swallowing a baby watersnake that slithered through the bayou. Here in the swamp, the black bear was king. Raider hoped he could avoid bumping into one of the burly creatures. A bear could take your head off with one swipe of his paw.

He stayed on high ground, walking the black stallion toward the north. Zavalla was one of the few towns Raider had never been in before. He wondered if he would be able to find it without asking directions. With a price on his head, every man jack would be trying to get off a lucky shot.

What the hell had Holt been thinking of anyway? A reputation was one thing, but a price was another. What if Starbin tried to kill him for the five hundred dollars?

He shook his head, disbursing the mosquitoes. He stunk so badly from the ride that he doubted they could get close enough to bite anyway. No need to stop for sleep, not as long as he didn't know where he was. Lost in east Texas—a hell of a predicament for a man who was used to finding his way around.

A tracker used everything at his disposal, Raider thought. Eyes, nose, ears. He had to stay alert to any trace that might lead him to where he was going. Raider heard the clinking of a blacksmith's hammer as it echoed over the treetops. He followed that sound until he could smell the smoke from the forge. Then he broke through the trees to see Zavalla standing like a rundown railroad station in the distance.

Of course, he could not ride into town, not with those damned wanted posters in circulation. Had somebody put them on a train or a stage? They had gotten east from Austin awfully quickly.

But at least he had a starting point now that he had reached Zavalla. He knew Starbin's spread was on the other side of the slapdash village, in the middle of the rich grasslands that bordered the Sabine River. Beyond Starbin's place were the northern reaches of the big swamp that Raider had encountered before. Not a place for a man who might have to get away fast. If he left in a hurry, he would have to go west, away from Zavalla.

Using what he could remember of the report from Forbin's office, Raider circled around the dismal hamlet, making for the edge of Starbin's property. He would have to be careful on his approach. A man who was up to no good would undoubtedly have sentries about his place. And Raider wanted to take a look before he tried to meet the colonel.

The black's hooves made deep prints in the soft, flat earth that stretched toward the Sabine. At first Raider thought the ground would not provide enough cover for a clandestine peek at the old rebel's property. But when he saw the line of trees in the distance, he figured that his luck had turned.

Raider dismounted in the stand of forest, peering toward a two-story house in the distance. A rail fence guarded the entrance to the colonial style mansion that was encircled by oak trees. Raider would have sworn he was in Georgia if he had not known better.

The big man did not have a spyglass but he could see the rough men who lingered by the front gate of the spread. Five of them. Two on the fence with rifles or shotguns and three on horseback. Not exactly the best situation for a tough stranger to ride into. What if they had orders to shoot on sight? Even Raider would have trouble with five men.

"Damn."

As he hooked his boot in the stirrup to remount, Raider heard the clicking of a well-oiled revolver. The gunman had come quietly out of nowhere. Cold iron pressed against the big man's neck.

"Lookin' for somebody?"

Raider knew the gunman was good so any move would have to be final. Maybe it was best just to play it out. Hell, the man hadn't shot him yet and he had gotten the drop on him without too much trouble.

"Heard the colonel was hirin'," Raider said. "They call me Buck. I'm lookin' for work."

"Buck, huh? You sure your name ain't lawman?"

Raider spat. "That's for lawman, pardner." He started to disengage his foot from the stirrup.

"Stay where you are," the gunman urged. "And keep them hands on the saddle horn. You might live if you stand still long enough."

Raider stayed still. "I like to see the man who's drawin' down on me, pardner. Like to face 'im head on."

"Give me a reason why I shouldn't kill a big ape like you."

"Fernandez sent me," Raider replied.

The cold steel left his neck.

Raider straightened himself and turned to look at the slender man who was smiling at him. A clean-cut cowboy dressed to wrangle. Tan hat. Clean-shaven face that wasn't too old. Big hands holding a .44 Remington, the same kind of pistol Raider had carried before he switched to the Colt.

"So Fernandez sent you," the cowboy said.

Raider nodded. He didn't like the loco grin on the young face. He had seen it before, the kid's stare; wild-eyed, ready to kill anybody who crossed him. The kind of man who never lost sleep after a gunfight.

"What do they call you?" Raider asked.

"Bake. Real name's Jimmy Baker, but I go by Bake."

Raider didn't like staring down the one-eyed bore of the Remington. "I'd be obliged if you holstered your friend there."

"And let you draw on me? Shit."

Raider shrugged. "Have it your way. I reckon you're the colonel's chief scout an' fast gun. I wouldn't wanna take your place. So I ain't got no reason to draw on you. Wouldn't want t' fight myself out of a job."

"Where'd you meet Fernandez?" the kid asked quickly.

"Beaumont."

"Where in Beaumont?"

"Mex town."

"What kind of hat was he wearin'?"

"Sombrero."

"He ask you for money?"

"Said he got it on this end," Raider replied.

Bake seemed satisfied. "Okay, we walk in. You first."

Raider started to grab the reins of the black.

"I'll take it," Bake said. "Don't want you pullin' no funny stuff."

Raider nodded at the Remington. "What about the hog-leg?"

Bake smiled. "It stays in my hand, big 'un. Any objections to that?"

Raider shook his head and turned toward the mansion.

The five sentries eyed Raider as he passed under the sign that proclaimed the spread to be the Double Star Ranch. This seemed like an unfitting name, as there were no stars or cattle to live up to the title. There were plenty of guns around, however. All five guards were packing shotguns and double pistols in their belts.

One of them exchanged glances with Bake.

"Fernandez sent him," the kid called back.

As they drew closer to the house, Raider could see that it was in a terrible state of disrepair. The paint was peeling and the shutters were all rotten or hanging by a single hinge. There was a smell of decay and mildew about the place. One of the high colonial columns had cracked in two on the veranda.

"Place needs a carpenter," Raider offered.

"Let's have all your guns," Bake said. "I know a man like you is bound to have more than one."

"Just the Colt and a derringer," Raider said, handing them both to the gunman. "I trust you're gonna give 'em back t' me."

"Maybe. You wouldn't have anything in your boot, would you?"

Raider gave him the hunting knife.

"Okay," Bake said finally, "let's go meet the colonel."

Raider was led through the dusty rooms of the old house. He wondered what it had looked like twenty years ago, before the war. Most of the downstairs rooms were not suited for living. You could have made a thousand bandages from the stringy cobwebs.

"Don't nobody ever sweep up 'round here?"

Bake laughed. "You're a real stitch, Mr. Buck. Hey, Bake and Buck. It's gonna be funny if we start workin' together."

Raider was startled when they entered a spotless study. Books lined the walls and new furniture graced the floor. Behind a large desk sat an ancient man, greyed and wrinkled like a corpse that Raider had once seen pulled out of the snow. When the old man opened his eyes, they were clotted and glassy.

"Who is it?" he asked.

The old bastard was blind.

"It's Private Baker," the kid replied.

Raider squinted at him. "Private?"

"Shh," Baker said. "Just play along."

"Any word from the front, Private?"

"No, sir, Colonel Starbin. A new recruit has arrived. Sergeant Buck. Mr. Fernandez sent him up from Beaumont."

Raider looked back and forth between the two men. "What in the name of God is . . ."

"Good afternoon, Sergeant Buck," Tanner Starbin said. "Excuse me if I don't get up. I don't see as well as I once did. Tell me, Buck. What do you think of this business of freeing the slaves?"

Raider's jaw slacked. The old boy was playing with fifty-one cards. He was even wearing his old gray uniform.

"Worst thing Lincoln ever did," Starbin went on. "Why, the nigger man is destined to serve the white man. It's God's law."

Bake nudged Raider with the barrel of the Remington. "Tell him you agree."

Raider said he agreed although it turned his stomach to say it.

"We're gonna put a stop to this Yankee nonsense," Starbin

said. "And I hope you're prepared to fight, Sergeant Buck."

Raider leaned closer to Bake's ear. "Thanks for makin' me a sergeant, Baker, but what the hell is goin' on here?"

"Shh. Just watch. Er, Colonel, where is Captain Starbin?"

"I'm right here, Baker."

Raider turned to see a man sitting in a wheelchair. A woman was pushing the chair through another door that opened into the study. Raider tried not to stare at her red hair and ample chest. Instead, he focused on the man in the rolling chair.

"I'm Bond Starbin," the man said. "This is Mrs. Starbin. Regina, will you take the colonel into the kitchen for something to eat?"

The expression on Regina Starbin's pretty face told Raider that she was not enthusiastic about handling the old man, but she did it anyway. Raider watched her shifting backside as she led him away. The colonel was raging against Grant and the "rest of those bluebellies." When they were gone, Raider turned his attention back to Bond Starbin.

"You must forgive my father," Starbin said. "He hasn't been well of late. Did I hear that your name is Buck?"

Raider shrugged. "It is for now."

He studied the shape of the man that Baker had called Captain Starbin. His skin was pale, as if he rarely saw the sun. Thin body, frail from lack of use. He couldn't walk and his daddy couldn't see. A fine pair. Certainly not the kind to threaten a whole state.

Starbin moved himself by handing the large wheels of the chair. He maneuvered around behind the desk, all the time watching Raider. Something was eerie about Starbin's eyes, the way they seemed deep and hollow. His hair had been slicked back like a stiff helmet. Black suit and ribbon tie. A plaid blanket covered his useless legs.

"Did you fight in the great conflict between the states, Mr. Buck?"

Raider shook his head. "I was too young."

Starbin nodded. "Yes, you would have been. I went to war when I was seventeen. Served under my father. A Yankee bullet cost me the use of my legs."

Raider just stood there, saying nothing.

"So Mr. Fernandez thought I might put you to work," Starbin said. "Well, he has sent me several good men. And now he's sending me a Pinkerton."

Baker bristled, thumbing back the hammer of the Remington. "A Pinkerton! I oughta plug you right now!"

Bond Starbin held up his hand. "Wait, Private Baker."

The son was using the army chatter too.

Starbin took something out of a desk drawer. "Here. When you see this you may change your tune, Baker."

He dropped the wanted poster on the desktop.

"Can you read, Private Baker?"

"Yes, sir."

"Then what does this say?"

It took him a moment, but Baker finally said, "He's wanted for killin' somebody in Austin."

"Precisely," Starbin replied. "He killed one of my enemies for me. A man named Forbin."

Raider glared at the man in the chair. "How long you had that?"

Starbin shrugged. "One of my men picked it up down in Woodville. You're a wanted man, Sergeant Raider."

"Ain't no sergeant," the big man replied.

Starbin frowned. "Then you don't want to come to work for me? You don't want to put that gun of yours to good use?"

Raider tried not to look too eager. "You mean you ain't gonna shoot me?"

Starbin laughed, a friendly, frightening chuckle. "I don't hurt men who help my cause, sir. You did me the biggest favor any man could do. And now you find your way into my house. Why, it would be less than honorable of me to turn you away in your time of need."

"But he's a Pinkerton!" Baker insisted.

"*Was* a Pinkerton," Raider rejoined. "I don't cotton t' that line o' work no more. Never did make enough t' buy myself a decent horse."

Baker wasn't buying it. "Oh yeah, where'd you get that stallion?"

"Read the poster," Starbin insisted. "He stole it. He's not only a murderer, he's a horse thief."

Raider kept thinking that Holt had done a good job with the wanted poster. Just the right touch. If Starbin hadn't seen it, the big man from Arkansas would probably have a bullet in his back by now.

Starbin nodded toward the door. "Take Mr. Raider and get him settled in, Private Baker."

"I thought I was a sergeant," the big man offered.

"So you are, Sergeant Raider. So you are. I hope you find our company to be suitable." Starbin started to wheel himself back toward the other door.

"Like to know what I'm signin' on for," Raider said quickly. "What's expected o' me 'round here?"

Starbin didn't even look back. "In due time, sir. In due time."

Baker was right beside him. "Here, take your guns. And I reckon I oughta say somethin' good about you hirin' on, but I ain't never cottoned to no Pinkertons. Not even one that's gone bad."

Raider wanted to say that he had never cottoned to outlaw scum, but he knew he had to hold his tongue.

As they were starting out, the woman stuck her head back into the study. "Bond?" She locked eyes with Raider. "Oh." Slight smile.

Then she was gone.

Raider recognized the look. A woman always checked out any new men that came into her territory. She approved. That might mean trouble later. Or it might mean a hell of a good time. And women liked to talk. They'd tell you things that could really help out in an investigation.

"Better stay away from that redheaded bitch," Baker offered.

"I will," the big man replied.

But even as he said it, he knew it was a lie.

CHAPTER FOURTEEN

As they came out onto the porch of the mansion, Raider noticed that the five sentries were standing next to his mount. They were examining the brand, wondering who it had been stolen from. When Raider started toward the animal, all five sets of eyes turned his way. One man squinted and then his face slacked into an expression of awe and surprise.

"It's Raider, that Pinkerton son of a bitch!"

The big man froze on the veranda, his hand dropping immediately to the butt of his Colt. His fingertips tickled the grip. The sentry who had spoken was also motionless.

Raider tried to diffuse the situation. "Goin' by the name Buck now, pardner. I'm on the same side of the law as you."

The sentry pointed a finger at him. "You sent me to Rock Springs up in Colorado. I almost rotted in the seven years I spent there. All them jailbirds tryin' to poke me in my ass."

Raider grinned, knowing the smile wouldn't work. "Hey, boy, what do they call you?"

He couldn't remember the face, just another outlaw he had taken in over the years. He couldn't recall what the man had done in the first place. Too many cases to remember them all.

One of the others tried to settle things a little. "Lay off him, Scoggins. He ain't the same man. Look at him."

Scoggins waved the man away. "I don't care if he signed in blood with the Devil himself. I swore when I got out of Rock Springs that I'd kill him. Every day I hurt in that prison hole, I told myself that one day I'd come eye to eye with the big ape. I've got to do it."

Baker stepped up next to the big man. "Scoggins, I don't like havin' him here any more'n you do. I ain't never took to no Pinks. But you saw the wanted poster. He's one of us now. Mr. Starbin done took him on."

"Then I'm gonna take him off," Scoggins replied.

Raider waved Baker away. "He wants t' do it, Bake. I'd rather face 'im head on than have 'im sneakin' up b'hind me."

Baker nodded, half-smiling like he didn't mind seeing a gunfight.

Raider looked at the other four gunmen. "This is b'tween Scoggins an' me, boys. If you want a little o' me afterwards, I'll be ready t' try you one at a time. Fists or sixguns. I ain't partic'lar."

They talked it over and then one of them said, "Scoggins, you're on your own. We can't help you."

The wild-eyed gunslinger spat in their direction. "To hell with all of you. I can take him. I been waitin' a long time for this day."

"We're ready to accept the winner," the man said to Raider. "No hard feelin's."

Raider said that was all right with him. Then he looked at Scoggins: "How you want it? Right here, or you wanna square off in the yard?"

Scoggins's face had turned bright red. He knew he couldn't back off now. Raider kept his eyes on the man's hands. Never look him in the face. He would shoot you with his eyes. Watch the hands, the slight twitch of first movement, the telltale quiver that let you know he was going to try it.

The others started to make bets, including Baker. It didn't matter to them who won. Scoggins obviously wasn't liked, so they didn't feel like they had to back him up. After all, he had issued the challenge, not Raider.

And the big man was pretty sure that Scoggins was their second top gun, after Baker who seemed to be respected as the fastest. A fight with Scoggins would give them an idea of how good the ex-Pinkerton actually was with his Colt. If Scoggins beat Raider to the draw, they were rid of him. And if Raider won, they'd know where he stood in the pecking order.

"What's it gonna be, Scoggins? Are you . . ."

The man's hand moved. Raider drew and pumped two shots into his chest, fanning him down before he could lift the old Navy Colt from his holster. Scoggins walked backward, falling into the dirt as the life ran out of him. He twitched for a while but he ultimately managed to die.

Raider stood there with the gun smoking in his hand. He had four shots left. There were five guns, counting Baker. If they wanted him gone, one of them could get him, maybe all of them.

But nobody wanted to die, at least not right away.

Baker was wide-eyed. "Scoggins didn't even clear leather."

"No, but he did draw first," one of the others chimed in.

"Yeah, he sure did."

Raider slipped the hogleg into leather. He hesitated with his arm hanging low. "Do it now, if you wanna try it. We ain't gonna have time for no nonsense later."

They were all smiling weakly.

"Don't nobody want to try you," Baker said.

"Too damned fast for me," replied one of the others.

Baker laughed. "Damn, it's a good thing you went bad, mister. I'd hate like all hell to have you chasin' me."

Raider walked off the porch, stepping over the body of the dead outlaw. The big man knew he should have felt bad about having to kill Scoggins, but somehow the remorse did not come. Maybe it was because he had other things to think about.

Baker gestured to the body. "Boys, get ol' Scoggins there in the ground. Put him deep so the bears don't dig him up."

Raider glared at the gunfighter. "Got a problem with bears, do you?"

Baker shrugged. "Sometimes. Had to shoot an old grandaddy bear the other day. He was coming up here after our goats."

"Goats?"

"Yeah, Miss Regina likes to use the milk."

Raider unhitched his horse from the post. "Reckon I'll make me a camp out in the woods."

He wanted to be free to operate.

Baker wasn't buying it. "Hell, you can sleep in the bunkhouse. There's two of them out behind the stable. Used to be slave quarters. Used to be a lot of cotton down this way."

Raider figured it would look suspicious if he decided to refuse the hospitality. After all, he was an employee of Tanner Starbin now. Or Bond Starbin—the son was really in control. And what about the woman?

"Why don't you take the one bunkhouse for yourself?" Baker offered.

Raider grimaced. "I thought there were a lotta men here."

"Not in the bunkhouses," was Baker's cryptic reply.

The big man figured it was best not to push for a more elaborate answer.

Baker rubbed the stallion's neck. "Good lookin' horse."

"I know a good mount when I steal one," Raider replied.

Baker rubbed his chin. "Seems like I've seen this horse before. And the brand too. Where'd you steal him?"

"Austin, just like the poster says."

"Oh yeah," Baker replied. "Say, the boss really was happy about what you done for him, killin' that Forbin, I mean."

"I reckon he was."

They started walking toward the bunkhouse. Raider looked back for a second to see a drape being pulled away from a window on the second story. It was the woman, staring out at him. She closed the drape when she saw his face turn toward her.

Raider smiled, wondering how long it would take for her to find him.

"Sergeant Raider," Baker said. "You like the sound of it?"

Raider frowned, shaking his head. "What the hell is all this military bull anyway? Last I heard, the Confederate Army died years ago."

"Don't fret," Baker replied. "You'll find out soon enough."

Raider found the bunkhouse to be equipped better than he could ever have expected. There was a smoked ham hanging from the ceiling and a bowl of eggs on a table. He lit the wood stove and started to melt lard in a big iron skillet. In no time at all he had filled his belly.

Then he knew he needed to have a bath. The woman wouldn't come to him if he was dirty. She had the hungry look. Maybe the Yankee bullet had taken more than Bond Starbin's legs.

He heated water and filled a small wooden tub.

After he had scrubbed off a layer of skin with lye soap, he boiled his clothes and hung them up to dry. Maybe he'd start wearing that new shirt, the one he had purchased back in Austin. Women liked new things.

He caught his reflection in a piece of mirror that hung on

the wall of the bunkhouse. He looked like something that had crawled out of the woods. The beard and the long hair had to go.

After sharpening the straight razor that he carried in his saddlebag, Raider lathered up and set to work stripping his face of the beard. He managed to get it down to a mustache and then decided to take that off. Who the hell was that in the mirror?

He looked younger without the whiskers.

Next he lopped off the long curls of hair that made him scraggly and unkempt. He had barbered himself before, so he was able to keep everything even. Raider would never think of himself as a handsome man, but he knew some of the ladies liked his face.

As he was rinsing soap away, he heard a horse galloping past the bunkhouse. He looked out the window expecting to see Baker or one of the other hands riding past. Instead, he got a glimpse of Regina Starbin bouncing in the saddle. She had changed into riding pants and a blouse. Where the hell was she going in such a hurry? Making to the east, toward the swamp.

Raider planned to follow her the first chance he got. For now it was better to stay put, get some rest, figure his moves before he started them. No reason to move too quickly, at least until he found out what was really going on.

Just before dusk, Raider was standing at the window of the bunkhouse, peering out into the shadows. He wore only his underpants, as his jeans and cotton shirt were not completely dry. While he was taking in the landscape, Regina Starbin rode through again, this time turning to see the big man in the window. Shc looked away quickly, like she was embarrassed.

Raider grinned and waved.

Mrs. Starbin went right on by.

"She's a beautiful woman, isn't she?"

Raider wheeled to see Bond Starbin sitting in a wooden chair. Baker stood beside him. Starbin had obviously been carried in by the hired gunman. Raider saw for the first time that the southern gentleman did not have any legs. His pants had been tied in knots over two stumps.

Starbin saw the big man staring at his infirmity. "Did I say a Yankee bullet took my legs? I meant a Yankee cannonball."

Raider didn't know what to say so he kept quiet.

"Mrs. Starbin is off limits, soldier."

Raider nodded. "I ain't much on women anyway. They cause a lot more trouble than they're worth."

Starbin patted his stumps. "I wear the wooden legs under my blanket," he offered. "I usually don't like to bother people with my deformity, but I had to come see you, Sergeant. I figure you to be a man of strong stomach."

"Mostly I am."

Starbin looked over his shoulder at Baker. "Private, will you leave us alone for a moment? I'll call you when I'm ready."

"Yes, sir."

Baker glared at Raider for a moment. "Better treat the boss good, Buck."

Raider nodded. "He's safe with me."

Baker left them alone.

Starbin sighed and then smiled weakly. "A good man, Baker. But he can be a little thick at times."

Raider pulled his longjohns up over his arms and chest. "I got the feelin' he's your top kick 'round here."

"He was," Starbin replied. "Until you arrived."

Raider wasn't sure how to take that.

"But you see," Starbin went on, "when you arrived, Sergeant, you created a big problem. I had the men all set to follow Baker and now you emerge as the fastest gunhand in camp."

"If you mean I shot Scoggins . . ."

Starbin waved him off. "Incidental. In fact, you did us all a favor. Scoggins wasn't a very good soldier. And I must wonder now how good a soldier you will be, Sergeant Raider."

Raider shrugged. "I'm as good as you need. An' better than you can get. It all depends on what you want me t' do. I ain't figurin' to ride blind into nothin'. You get my drift, Captain?"

Starbin smiled, appreciating Raider's forcefulness. "You're aggressive. I like that. And you'll know what's expected of you in due time. You see, Sergeant, I plan to build the whole squad around you. You'll be the core of it. The strength. The others will follow you into Hell if they have to."

"I ain't plannin' t' wind up six feet under, Captain."

"Good. I like your confidence. I hope it's catching. The others certainly need a bit more spirit. After all, a mercenary army can't be expected to fight as well as a force built of native sons. Look at the Romans. The minute they couldn't defend themselves, their civilization fell apart."

Raider wasn't sure about Romans. He only wanted to be rid of the captain so he could start poking around, taking his bearings. And the thing with the woman was going to be tricky. Even if Starbin couldn't satisfy her, he was probably watching her closely enough to make sure nobody else was doing it either. Raider still couldn't believe that the legless man was a threat to the security of the Lone Star state.

Starbin was glaring at him. "So, we understand each other, Sergeant?"

Raider exhaled, shaking his head. "I keep hearin' a lotta bull 'bout armies an' such. Only, you got five men out there. I don't see how you think that five men makes a militia."

"A good officer keeps many secrets," Starbin replied. "He doesn't tell his left hand what his right hand is doing. Nor the reverse. You see, Sergeant, you're going to be my right hand when I get through with you. Private Baker will call for you tomorrow morning. Until then, I suggest you get some sleep. You're going to need it."

Raider figured he had better say something about pay. "What's my draw on this deal, Starbin?"

"Captain Starbin."

"All right, Captain Starbin, what's my . . ."

"Ten dollars a day," Starbin replied. "I'll pay you forty dollars at the end of the week and the rest when the mission is completed."

Raider knew he couldn't argue with that. "I just hope you got the money, Captain. I know you ain't wastin' it on your house."

"You'll get your money, Sergeant. I'll pay you more than you ever hoped to earn working for the Pinkertons."

"I'll hold you t' that."

Starbin called for Baker who transported him outside to his wheelchair.

Raider watched them as they headed back for the house. What the hell was that crippled man up to? He certainly didn't seem to be letting his handicap stop him from making all kinds of trouble. And that crazy talk about slaves and the army. Hadn't the Starbins heard that the war had been over for years? Hell, as far as Raider knew, most of the troops had already been removed from the south. And the rest of them weren't far behind. President Hayes had seen to that.

The big man shook his head, feeling the first chill of evening. It was November after all. The cold weather could set in at any time. It didn't snow much in east Texas, but it could get chilly in the winter.

He took his damp clothes and put them on the stove until they were dry.

When he was dressed again, he went outside to turn his attention to the main house. A lamp burned in the window of the woman's room. Raider could see her walking back and forth as she paced there.

Why did he feel so drawn to her? It was more than her buxom form. She seemed to be trapped, like a spirited animal in a cage.

Raider started for the house, but by the time he slid up next to the wall, the Starbins were embroiled in a heated argument.

"Stay away from him," Bond cried. "I'll hurt you if you don't."

The woman said something but a slapping sound cut her words short.

Raider wondered if Starbin had Baker doing his slapping for him.

"You're crazy, Bond," Regina shouted at her worthless husband. "I never even looked at him. He's a saddle tramp."

"I'll kill you both!" the irate husband cried.

Raider figured he had better wait awhile before he tried to corner the lady of the house. He wondered how deeply involved she was. Maybe she didn't want to be in on the scheme—whatever it was.

Back in the bunkhouse, Raider stretched out on a bed, trying to sort it all out. The crazy father and son seemed to be preparing for some kind of maneuver, but where and why? Raider needed answers in a hurry. Then he had to get word to the authorities, to the home office. What if the damned thing was too big for a whole squad of Pinkertons? The regular militia and the cavalry would have to be called in.

Tossing in the bunk, Raider waited for sleep to come. He kept thinking about the woman. But he didn't imagine himself in bed with her. Instead, he pictured that troubled look on her face—like somebody in over her head.

Finally he dropped off, only to be awakened by the sound of a horse's hooves as it flew by his window at dawn.

Raider sat up to see Regina Starbin riding to the east again.

He got out of bed, expecting to follow her. But by the time he was dressed, Baker was at the door, calling him out. There was work to be done, the cowboy said. And Sergeant Raider had better hurry.

That morning, they drilled like soldiers, marching in single file to the commands of Captain Starbin who sat by in his chair.

Raider sort of liked the marching. He had never gotten a chance to be a soldier and he prided himself on doing it right. Starbin seemed to be pleased with his progress as the morning wore on.

The afternoon brought bayonet drills and target practice. Raider proved himself to be a crack shot with his Winchester. Again Starbin commended him on his skill.

Just as Raider figured the day was winding down, the real drills began. This time it was on horseback. At first they were just riding between barrels, making their mounts take sharp turns. Ride hard in and out of the barrels, then wheel around and dig in the opposite direction. Raider found the black to be good at anything he wanted him to do.

Then came the rifle shooting from horseback. They'd run between the barrels toward a straw-man figure with a piece of wood where the heart should be. Starbin ordered them to fire at the straw-man, aiming for the heart. He promised a dollar for every time they hit the wood.

The others had obviously been practicing as they hit the target on the second or third try.

Starbin smirked at Raider when his turn came. "Let's see how good you are with that rifle when you're on the run."

Raider put his Winchester back in the scabbard on his sling ring. "I don't need no rifle, Captain. Watch this."

"He'll never do it," Baker said.

"I'll bet he can."

"You're on."

Raider spurred the stallion and galloped toward the straw-man. When he was in range, he drew his Colt and fired twice.

The first bullet knocked the wooden heart in the air, the second shot split it into two pieces. Raider wheeled on the black and came back between the barrels.

Starbin applauded him. "Very good. I knew you were the one I had been looking for. Excellent."

Raider reined up, sliding out of the saddle, holstering his smoking Colt. "So I reckon you hired me t' kill somebody, Captain. Only thing is, I'd like t' know who I'm gonna kill."

"In due time," Starbin replied. "Private Baker, will you please push me back to the house?"

Raider watched them go. The captain seemed to know his business. Hell, a snake didn't have any legs and it could get around all right. It could strike and kill you, too.

"Some fine shootin'," said one of the other men.

"Yeah, I never seen anything like it."

Raider glared back at them. "I had a lotta practice."

"Bet you have."

Raider wondered if the others knew any more than him. "Captain there ain't big on tellin' us much. Is he?"

"Don't pay to ask too many questions when you're gettin' five dollars a day," replied one of his colleagues.

Raider was getting double the going rate; Starbin thought that much of his abilities. "You boys seen any o' that money?" the big man asked.

"Seen plenty," one of them replied. "Hey, big 'un, what are you gripin' about? You get your own bunkhouse."

"Ain't complainin'," Raider rejoined. "It's just that, well, any man payin' good wages like this must have somethin' he wants done pretty bad."

"Who cares what it is?" another man said. "I know he's only payin' the boys in the swamp a dollar a day. And we got it a lot better'n they do, I can tell you that."

"I don't care who it is he wants killed," offered the first man, "At this price, I plan on gettin' the job done."

Raider agreed it was good pay, but added, "I'd just like to know when, where, an' how. Don't like bein' kept in the dark. Too many things can go wrong."

"I heard Captain Starbin say somethin' about before Christmas," one of them offered. "But that don't mean nothin'. He likes to talk in code."

Raider figured he had stretched it about as far as he could.

"I'm headin' in for a bath an' some food. Anybody wanna join me?"

They all said they had other things to do.

Scared of the new man. They had seen him draw on Scoggins. They knew they weren't fast enough to take him. Raider wondered if they had any ideas about shooting him in the back for the reward money.

That poster was still a pain, even if it had helped him. He couldn't forget which side of the fence he was on. Until the matter at hand was cleared up, Raider was still an outlaw.

He had more ham and eggs.

After dinner he took a cold bath and shaved again.

He made sure he was standing in the window with his shirt off when the woman rode by that evening. She had been in the swamp all day. She still looked pretty good. When she saw Raider, she reined up and stopped for a moment.

He nodded to her. "Evenin', ma'am."

Her blouse was soaked with perspiration. He could see the circles of her pink nipples beneath the fabric. Her chest rose and fell as she looked at him. She nodded slightly and then rode off again toward the house.

The nod had been an invitation. Raider knew he would have to go in late, after everyone was asleep. She probably didn't sleep in the same bedroom with her husband. He wondered if he could pull it off.

Raider had never been much for carrying on with other men's wives, but he knew if he was going to get to the bottom of things, he had to become better acquainted with Regina Starbin.

CHAPTER FIFTEEN

Raider sat in the shadows, watching the dark house, wishing he had not thrown away the bottle of whiskey. He had ventured as far as the big pecan tree. It was the last place to hide before he had to run straight for the back door. Baker would probably be around, as well as the four men who always seemed to be close to the captain.

The big man still had to wonder about all of the military stuff. From what he could see, the pride of Dixie wasn't much anymore, at least not in fielding an army. But Forbin's man had reported a strong force of men, at least thirty of them. Hadn't one of the hands made a remark about the boys in the swamp getting paid a dollar a day?

Who the hell was out there anyway?

Regina Starbin would know. If he ever got to her. A lamp still burned low in the kitchen. It had been steady and there hadn't been any shadows flickering back and forth on the wall.

What if a man with a shotgun was sleeping in the pantry? Raider had been all alone in the bunkhouse. He really wasn't sure where any of the other men slept at night.

Raider figured he had to try it sooner or later. Maybe he'd get so far and stop. Make an excuse for why he was in the kitchen. Came to look for salt and whiskey.

He kept thinking about the woman, the desperate look in her eyes, like somebody who had boarded a boat to Hell and wanted to get off. She had ridden into the swamp two days in a row. She would have an idea of what was out there.

Crouching low, he left the cover of the tree, heading straight for the kitchen door. He was barefooted for silence, so his feet caught every stone and pebble in the yard. He was pretty sure a chicken with a bowel problem had also been in the area.

Easing onto the back steps, he caught his breath, listening. Was that a sentry snoring? Or the purring of a cat?

Raider started to raise up.

Shadows flickered on the wall.

He froze until he realized that she had seen him.

They stared at each other for a few moments before she nodded.

She didn't look hungry anymore, only frightened. A modest robe covered her full figure. Red hair tied up in a bun behind her head. No rouge or powder. Mrs. Starbin hadn't come to play.

Raider reached for the door.

She shook her head, coming forward to turn down the lamp. When the room was dark, she eased the door open and came out onto the steps. Raider started to speak. Regina put her fingers on his lips.

"Out there," she whispered.

Raider took her hand and led her toward the pecan tree.

Regina matched his stride as if her life depended on it.

When they came close to the tree, Raider slid his arm around her waist. He tried to pull her close, to kiss her. Regina pushed him away.

"No, that's not what I want."

Raider smiled. "Not at all?"

"You fool. I misjudged you."

She started to walk away.

Raider grabbed her arm. "That perfume. You wore it for me. You knew I'd come. That's why you nodded at me this afternoon."

She looked back to glare at him. Her pretty face seemed flawless in the dark. "This isn't about perfume or about what I want, Mr. Pinkerton. If you don't know that, then I pity you."

He let go of her. "Okay, you're right. It ain't professional-like. But you gotta answer a few questions for me, lady."

Regina nodded, turning toward him. "Then I was right. You aren't really an outlaw."

"How'd you figure it?" he asked her.

"I don't know," she replied sadly. "I just saw something there. And then when I heard you were a Pinkerton . . . I don't know, I thought you were my only ray of hope. Tell me that you'll help me get out of here."

Raider knew it wasn't an act. She was trembling. He took her in his arms and held her gently. Regina began to cry.

He stroked her head. "You gotta hold up, girl. You were right on one thing. This ain't 'bout me an' you."

He pushed her gently away from his body.

"I'll help you," he said. "But you gotta help me, too."

"Anything," she said. "Anything at all."

She put her hand on his shoulder but he took if off. "It cain't be like that," the big man said. "I woulda done it t' get information, if I had knowed that was what you wanted. But now we gotta work t'gether."

"How? How?"

He exhaled dejectedly. "I don't rightly know. First thing you can do is tell me what you're doin' in the swamp every day."

"All right," she took a deep breath, bracing herself. "It's not much, believe me. I just ride out there in the morning to wait for the boats."

"What kinda boats?"

She shrugged. "Long, flat, wooden. Two of them. They come every day, twice. I just sit there and wait."

"What happens when the boats git there?"

"We load them, or rather, two men do. They're swamp people. They've lived out there all their lives. Bond pays them enough so they'll work for him, but he can't get them to leave the swamp."

Raider nodded. "Ain't that unusual. They're like mountain men only they got a bog 'stead of a mountain."

She laughed a little. "I never thought of it like that."

"What are you loadin' onto the boats?"

"Small packages," she replied. "Heavy but small. Lots of them. I've been down there for two weeks but the pile of stuff we're loading doesn't seem to get any smaller."

"He's shippin' it a piece at a time," Raider said. "But where? Is this stuff goin' out into the swamp?"

"I'm not sure," she replied. "It could be. Or . . ."

"Don't hold back, honey. I gotta know whatever you can tell me."

She sighed. "Well, I've heard the men talk. They talk

about two canals. One leads into the swamp, one leads into the lake."

"Lake? What lake?"

"I don't know the name," she said. "It goes a long way, almost to the Louisiana border. At least that's what I've heard."

Raider studied on it. Two little boats, taking small loads across the lake to something else. The army maybe? He had to have a look at things himself. But first things first.

He took her arms and peered into her eyes. "Regina, you gotta tell me what your husband and your daddy are up to."

She scowled at him. "He ain't my daddy. And he ain't my husband, except in name and law. He's only got half a . . ."

She began to tremble.

He hugged her again. He was trying not to notice her perfume, but the scent worked its inevitable magic. Regina pressed hard against him, feeling his excitement.

"Thank you," she said. "I haven't felt like a woman in so long. Do you think I'm pretty?"

"Yes."

"I married quite young, you know. Before Bond went off to war. He was . . . well, he wasn't like he is now."

Raider pushed her away again. "Regina, you gotta tell me what they're plannin'. You been 'round it. What're they after?"

She gulped air, almost going limp. "I don't know. The guns, the powder. All that lead. I don't know. I keep hearing them talk about Shreveport."

"Louisiana?"

"I reckon."

He shook his head. "Some people thought old Tanner there wanted to pick a fight with the state o' Texas."

She laughed cynically. "They couldn't whip Zavalla. Much less the whole state."

"But all that artillery."

"They're sendin' it away," she said.

Raider touched her hand. "I wanna go out there t' see it myself. But they got me doin' that crazy drill. You know anythin' 'bout that?"

"Seems like you're going to kill somebody," she said. "That's all I know. But I say this, Mr. Pinkerton. Bond is leavin' tomorrow to go into Zavalla. He's going to be there all morning. If you want to see what's goin' on in the swamp, you better go then."

"What time is he leavin'?"

"Right after dawn."

He nodded hopefully. "Okay, that's fine. Are you goin' out t' the dock t'morrow?"

"Yes."

"I'll foller b'hind you," he said. "I should be able to . . ."

She stopped him. "Shh. Go."

"But . . ."

A lamp went on upstairs.

"Back to the bunkhouse," she urged. "I'll see you in the morning."

She ran quickly toward the mansion.

Raider watched her as she sidled up to the back porch.

The lamp came down the stairs. Baker was carrying Bond Starbin. It was a pitiful sight. But Regina played it carefully.

Before they could get downstairs, she bounced into the kitchen and started to fool around with something. Then she came back out again, bending over to pour something into a saucer. Before her husband could holler at her, she looked back and told him she was feeding the cat. Her luck held when a white cat seemed to come out of nowhere.

Raider swung around and headed back to the bunkhouse.

When he was in bed, he tried to sort it out. At least the woman was helping him. She wanted out, and rightly so. Whatever her husband and her father-in-law had in mind, it was loco enough to repel her. Raider had seen many a woman go bad for a man. But Regina had strength and a good streak inside her. He just wished her perfume hadn't lingered all around him.

He tried not to think about her. Instead, he thought about her husband. Bond Starbin was a character all right—a dangerous one. Raider doubted much complicity by the old man. Tanner Starbin was little more than a blind turnip-head. The man with no legs had arranged nearly everything.

Before he fell asleep, the big man arrived at the conclusion that Bond Starbin didn't deserve a woman like Regina.

Raider's eyes popped open when he heard the footsteps outside the bunkhouse. Reflexively, he reached for the Colt rested beside him on the bed. He always slept with his gun close by. It made for staying alive a lot longer.

The steps were tentative. Maybe Bond Starbin had seen Raider and Regina together. Now he was sending Baker to do his dirty work for him, to shoot the big man while he slept.

Raider got up, sliding cautiously toward the door. Maybe Baker had the others with him for help. It would take more than one gunhand to get rid of the tall, irate Pinkerton.

He paused by the door, listening as the soft steps grew closer. He had to hand it to Baker, he was quiet. But not as quiet as the Indian who had taught Raider to be sneaky.

The footfalls halted for a few moments before they started up the steps to the bunkhouse entrance.

Raider flung open the door and leveled the Colt at the scared face. "You!"

Regina Starbin put a finger to his lips. "I don't want him to hear. He just got back to sleep. He'll be out till dawn."

Raider looked up at the dark sky. The air was chilly. He waved her into the bunkhouse.

"You took a big chance sneakin' out here," he offered.

"No more than you took to come here to stop Bond."

Raider caught a whiff of her perfume. She was now dressed in a frilly black robe. Her hair had been taken down, falling over her shoulders.

"I thought we were gonna let it ride," the big man said.

She lowered her eyes, sighing. "Do you know what it's like to live with somebody who doesn't want you? Somebody who couldn't do anything about it even if he wanted to."

Raider wasn't sure how he felt about the situation.

"And he won't let me near other men," she replied. "He's jealous. I . . . I was lying there in my bedroom, thinking. I decided to do something about it. I remembered how you were hard when you pressed against me."

That damned perfume and the red hair had him addled. "Regina, I don't think we . . ."

She dropped the robe and threw her naked body against him. "I want it, Raider. Please. I don't care if Bond finds out. I don't care what happens."

Her hungry mouth pressed against his. Raider felt the rising in his long johns. Her large breasts rubbed his chest, setting him afire.

"Damn it, woman."

"Yes, I'm a woman. And I want you."

Her hand clasped his prick, jerking him.

"Lie down," she urged. "Hurry. God, I'm so wet I'm dripping down my own thighs. Please."

Raider figured it was best to do as she said. Besides, he had to admit that he wanted it as bad as she did. He moved toward the bed, holding her, lying back on the cornhusk mattress.

Regina tore away his long johns, gripping his prick.

"Oh God," she moaned, "it's so big."

She straddled him, guiding the tip of his cock to her wet entrance. In one motion, she sat down, taking in his length. He was tight inside her.

Regina gasped for breath. Her whole body trembled with the penetration. She started to work her hips up and down, but finally her body would not cooperate. She had gone limp with her first release.

"Don't shoot yet," she said. "Please."

Raider touched her breasts, stroking the soft skin. "Here, it's time for you t' lay down."

Quickly they changed places. Raider's cock came out of her as they shifted. When he settled into the notch between her legs, she grabbed him and guided him back in.

"Slow," she said. "I want to enjoy it."

Raider obliged her. He moved his hips up and down, working his length in and out of the moist opening. Regina continued to tremble with each deliberate thrust, gasping and sobbing her completed joy.

"So long," she said. "It's been so long."

"You want me to pull out when I shoot?"

She shook her head. "No. Leave it in. As deep as you can get it. I want to feel it inside me."

He picked up his motion.

"Faster," she cried.

He obeyed her command.

"Harder."

He felt himself starting to rise.

She put her hand over her mouth, muffling her screams.

"Oh, God. Oh God."

Raider burst without warning, burying his prick to the hilt.

Regina grabbed his shoulders, pulling him down, kissing

his face. "I'm glad I changed my mind," she said. "That felt so good."

Raider started to pull out but she wouldn't let him.

"Just leave it in a little longer."

"We cain't be at this all night," he said. "What if your husband finds us here?"

"He'll kill us," she replied. "Dead as doornails. But I don't care."

Raider slid out finally. "Well, I ain't got any plans for dyin'. You better get back t' the house."

Even in the dark, he could tell she had started to pout.

"You don't want me?" she asked.

Raider exhaled. "That ain't the point."

"Please, just kiss my breasts. Touch them too. Just for a little while. Then I'll go."

She sounded so pitiful that he gave in.

His mouth found the firm rings of her aureoles, licking and sucking at the nippled ends.

Regina squirmed with the renewed attentions. She grabbed his sagging prick and gave it a couple of jerks. Raider came to life again.

"Lady. . ."

"Just once more," she said. "Please. It's been so damned long."

What the hell, he thought, he was hard again.

Regina spread her thighs, eagerly accepting him. Raider thrust in and out of her, waiting for his second release. When it came, he buried his cock again, wondering if anybody had heard the sounds of rapture that escaped from Regina's throat.

Their bodies were covered with sweat from the coupling. Regina sucked air, trying to find her breath. She didn't have much energy left in her body. Raider had drained most of that.

"Thank you," she said finally.

Raider slid out of her and sat up on the edge of the bunk. "You better git goin'. And try not to let any o' the other boys see you when you sneak back t' the house."

"This doesn't change things," she said. "You're still going to try to help me. Aren't you?"

"Just like we planned," he replied. "I'll follow you t' the swamp in the mornin' after Bond leaves."

She got up to retrieve her robe.

"Regina?"

She turned to look at him. "What?"

"You're a damned fine woman. I just hope I can get you outta all this. You deserve better."

She took a step toward him.

"No, just go back t' the house."

"All right."

She left without another word.

Raider watched from the bunkhouse window until she was inside the house. Then he went back to bed and slept soundly until he heard the rattling harnesses of Bond Starbin's carriage, departing on schedule at dawn.

As soon as Starbin was gone, Regina Starbin set out on her mount, heading straight for the swamp. Raider had dressed by then. He waited until she was out of sight before he went to saddle his horse.

As he was cinching the saddle on the stallion, one of the other men came up behind him. "Goin' somewhere, Buck?"

Raider tossed the reply over his shoulder as he swung into the saddle. "Figgered t' go shoot me a gator for supper. I like gator meat. How 'bout you?"

The man scratched his head. "Bake says we're supposed to drill today."

"Is Bake here?"

The man said that Baker had gone with Captain Starbin.

"Don't worry," Raider replied. "I'll be back afore you know it."

He spurred the black and dug headlong for the swamp.

He didn't follow Regina's tracks right away. Instead, he swung in a wide circle so it would appear to anyone watching from the house that he had gone in the opposite direction. When he was out of view, he doubled back and picked up her trail. It wasn't hard to follow. The earth was soft, leaving tracks that were as good as any roadmarker.

There were also deep ruts from wagons that had been back and forth between the house and the swamp. Someone had spread white sand to make the road firmer. The wagon tracks indicated that hundreds of trips had been made. Starbin was taking the hard way around, but the big man figured the captain probably had a good reason for it.

The trail began to narrow and the wagon tracks disappeared. Hoofprints replaced the ruts where the wagon could not go. Dark trees loomed overhead and the backwaters of the swamp rose up to mark the beginning of the morass. Raider felt a chill down his spine. A swamp could be a dangerous place. Too many critters that could bite you, some that might even kill you.

He reined up, slowing the black.

Suddenly he heard the sounds of the bog as it came to life in the morning air. A cottonmouth moccasin slithered across the path, startling the stallion. Raider had to get down to lead the animal by the reins.

Something grunted in the trees. Rustling through bushes. Was it a black bear scurrying away from the human scent? Or a white-tailed swamp buck running for cover?

Raider realized he had drawn his Colt. He holstered it, continuing on the trail as it grew narrower. Water surrounded him now. And the path started to wind with sinuous curves.

Another snake slithered off into the water. Raider felt like shooting it, but he didn't want to make a ruckus. Gunshots might scare away the boatmen if they were coming like Regina said.

"Raider! Over here!"

She was standing at the edge of a makeshift dock that had been lashed together out of rough cypress logs. Beside her rose a pile of goods that had been covered with a canvas tarp. Raider wondered how the dock supported the weight of the load.

He tied up the black and stepped over next to her. "The boatmen come yet?"

She shook her head. "They probably won't be here for a while."

"Good. I want to look under this tarp."

They peeled off the canvas to reveal the cargo underneath.

Raider tipped back his Stetson. "Lordy. Where did he get all this stuff? Cannonballs, powder, fuse cord. Coupla boxes o' dynamite."

"He stole it," Regina replied. "Where, I don't know."

Raider shook his head. "From an armory in Dallas," he replied. "Look here. It's marked on some o' the crates. But how? Those five idiots at the house couldn't have pulled this off. Unless . . ."

"What?"

Raider looked toward the channel that led into the marsh.

"Maybe the real power is on the other side. You ever see more'n five or six men 'round here?"

She thought about it for a while. "A couple of weeks ago, there was a big commotion in the middle of the night. I thought more men were coming through but Bond wouldn't let me out of my room."

Raider exhaled. "What the hell is he doin'? Draggin' all this hardware through the muck. Hell, it makes sense in a way. Nobody would see him out here. But what's he really up to?"

She slid next to him, putting her hand on his shoulder. "You were wonderful last night."

"Pretend it never happened," he replied. "At least for now."

She backed away, looking hurt.

"Don't go sour on me," Raider warned. "I'm gonna need your help. I heard one o' the hands mention somethin' 'bout before Christmas. You know anythin' 'bout that?"

She shrugged.

"What's today?"

"The second of December."

Raider shook his head. "Ain't cold 'nough for December. Damn." He was getting ready to ask her about the boatmen but he never got the chance.

Regina perked up, looking at the dark canal. "Shh. I think I hear them coming. You better hide."

He slipped back into the bushes with the chiggers and the dog flies.

The boatmen approached silently, mooring their long, flat-bottomed craft against the dock. Raider watched as they loaded a few pieces of cargo into their boats. Then they started back down the canal, making for what appeared to be the heart of the swamp.

When they were out of sight, the big man went back to the dock. "I gotta go after 'em, honey. Is there a boat 'round here?"

Regina pointed behind the pile of munitions. "Only a small rowboat. But it has oars."

"That's good enough."

They launched the rickety craft into the black water.

As Raider started to get in, Regina stopped him. "I want to go with you," she said. "I don't want to stay here alone."

He touched her cheek. "I like your courage, girl. But you gotta foller your reg'lar duties. And if anybody asks, you ain't seen me t'day. Got it?"

She gave him a kiss before he got behind the oars.

Raider rowed for a long time, knifing through the channel. He had to keep looking behind him to take his bearings. He hesitated when he saw that the canal split off into two forks.

"Damn."

He was pondering which stream to take when he saw the lump of metal sticking out of the water. When he drew closer, he realized it was a Stokes mortar that had not made it out of the swamp. The damned thing had sunk the boat that was carrying it.

The mortar was resting in the channel that veered to the right.

Right was the way to go.

Raider eased up on the oars, letting the current take him as fast as it would flow.

CHAPTER SIXTEEN

Raider steadied the small vessel with the oars, holding it straight as the current of the creek swept him out into the black water of the lake. He had to pick up the rowing again when the flow of the stream dissipated in the main body of water. The sun had risen overhead, warm and threatening for December. Sweat began to pour off his brow. He had to remove his coat and his leather vest.

When he was more comfortable, he rowed again, steering offshore to have a look. He stopped, taking in the coastline of the lake. Thick trees seemed to gird the entire bank, at least as far as he could see. Water birds stabbed for minnows among the lily pads while watersnakes slithered around in the new sun. To the north, a black bear emerged from the trees to drink at the water's edge.

Raider wondered if it was the same bear he had heard earlier. Black bears weren't as big as grizzlies or brown bears, but they could be just as mean when you cornered them. Most bears wouldn't hurt you though, as long as you left them alone.

The big man sighed. Plenty of wildlife around but no men in flat-bottomed boats. They had gotten away fast. *If* they had followed the creek into the lake. Maybe Regina had been wrong. Maybe they were taking the stuff deeper into the swamp. No, that didn't make sense, not if what they were planning was going to take place in Louisiana. Hadn't Regina said Shreveport?

He turned to peer toward the other side of the lake. He could barely see the opposite shoreline. That meant the lake had to be at least five or six miles across. How had the boatmen gotten out of sight so fast? He wasn't that far behind them. But then again, they were swamp people, more versed in the ways of water travel. Raider just had to put his back into it.

He rowed for a while in the hot sun, sweating through his shirt. So he took it off until the skin on his back started to burn. Too damned hot for December. He dipped the shirt in the lake and put it back on.

Where the hell were those men anyway? He gazed over his shoulder, realizing that he could now see the clear image of a shoreline in the distance. The other side was flat and low, which made it blend in to the horizon better than hilly terrain. Nothing to do but keep rowing.

As midday approached, he had to dip his hat in the lake. It was the only way to keep his head cool, even though he hated to do it. A wet hat lost most of its shape in a hurry.

More rowing. The other shoreline was now more apparent against the glow of the sun on the water. A few trees had popped up. And there was a boat coming straight for him. Raider stood up. Two boats were heading his way. Two flat-bottomed boats with swamp men sculling them as fast as they could go. Twice as fast as the rowboat. Raider watched them, tipping his hat when they had grown closer.

"Howdy, boys. Any catfish bitin'?"

Neither man replied. They went right on by, not even looking in his direction. Like he wasn't there.

Raider grinned, picking up the oars. They were quick enough that they would be back soon. Hadn't Regina said they made two trips a day? Raider figured he could slide onto the other shore to watch for their return. He'd mark where they landed and pay a little visit after they were gone.

Not a bad plan at all.

Just keep rowing.

And try not to curse the sun for being too hot in December.

Raider pulled the boat onto the muddy bank. He gazed at the low brush lands that stretched away from the water. A quick walk south didn't give up much, just more mud that was hard to trudge through. He wasn't sure why he thought the boatmen had come from somewhere south of where he had landed, but his instincts told him the cut across the lake had almost been a straight line for them. He had gone north a little so he could watch from afar.

Back at the boat, he wondered if he should pull the small craft into the bushes to hide it. But it was too heavy in the mud when he finally tried to drag it further on shore. He had to cut branches from low bushes to cover the vessel. After he had it hidden, he decided the blind stuck out just as much as the boat so he took the branches away.

While he toiled over the boat, he looked down to discover some cotton fishing twine and a small hook under the lone seat. Raider had never been much of a fisherman but he managed to cut a pole and catch a few grasshopers for bait. In a half hour he caught three sunfish and a small bass. Using some of the twigs from the branches he had cut, he fashioned a spit for the fish. He built a fire and roasted them until they were done enough to eat. Fish wasn't exactly his favorite, but he needed strength if things got hairy.

He wondered if the boatmen would see the smoke from the fire. Maybe there were others around who might see it. After all, the swamp people weren't sculling across the lake for their health. They were delivering their cargo to someone.

So he kicked out the fire and waited.

Where the hell were those peckerwoods? Maybe they would only do one load today. At this rate, it would take them a lifetime to whittle down the pile of scrap that Starbin had stored up.

After studying on it a while, Raider found some shade in the brush. He continued to roll it over in his head. First off, he had underestimated the man in the wheelchair. What was it that the report had said about Starbin's money? Hadn't it all come from cotton and corn?

Money. That was what allowed the man with no legs to buy his way around into no good. He was hiding behind his daddy, pretending to keep something alive that had died fifteen years before at Appomattox. Raider had never cared much about money. If he had a dollar or a hundred in his pocket it was all the same to him. Only a weak man would let money rule him.

The big man sat up quickly and listened to the breeze. What the hell was it that he had been hearing and not hearing since he pulled up on the muddy bank? Something tinged in the air, like a hammer on metal. But he didn't really hear it, did he? Like a blacksmith's peen on an anvil.

But he didn't hear it for certain so he leaned back against the shady bush.

There was something else to consider as well. Maybe Starbin wasn't the head honcho of this thing, whatever it was. Maybe he was just one of the pawns on the chess board. Still, it took a lot of guts to attempt to . . . Raider wasn't even sure what was being attempted.

As he thought more and more, it bothered him that he had come this far without any answers. And those damned boatmen were nowhere in sight. All he had were the stolen munitions, which were really enough to put Starbin away. Even if his trek across the lake gave up a big goose egg, he could still go back to Beaumont to alert the marshal. Get off a wire to the home office and to Peter Holt. Maybe it was best to end it that way.

But something told him that he had better wait.

He stared out across the lake, watching as the afternoon shadows lengthened. Still no boatmen. Maybe they were just too lazy to work. He felt pretty lazy himself. The air was beginning to cool a little. Nice songs of birds as they flitted through the brush.

When his eyes got heavy, he stood up and stretched.

Then he thought about the report he had read in Forbin's dim office. The man from the justice department had seen a lot of men busy at some task. "Like an army at work." Hadn't those been the exact words?

There didn't seem to be much evidence of that so far.

And what was all that bull about Christmas? Raider counted the days. If something happened before, that gave him just a couple of weeks.

He made the mistake of sitting back down.

His eyes continued to watch the lake but his mind started to wander. He let himself think about Regina, the way she had come to the bunkhouse in her frilly robe. Then he was there with her, replaying it all again in a dream.

But something went wrong in his reverie and he snapped awake to the mosquitoes that buzzed in the east Texas dusk.

"That was real bright," he said to himself.

If the boatmen had come, he had missed them.

Falling asleep was about the stupidest thing he could have done. Or so he thought until he heard the strange noise. It was louder than the sound he had imagined before. Almost like a dull roar.

He came down out of the brush to launch the boat. His feet

got wet but he was soon on the lake again, rowing in the dark. The mosquitoes followed him like hungry vultures.

As he moved out further into the lake, Raider saw the glow on shore. A shining yellow halo of light seemed to rise up out of the brush. He also saw smoke and sparks from the mouth of some kind of brick chimney. There was no doubt in his mind that he had found what he was looking for. It burned like the storm lamp on Satan's front porch.

Now all he had to do was get to it in the dark.

On the approach to the shoreline, Raider squinted in the darkness, straining to see what he believed to be the mouth of a creek. He figured the inlet was the place where the boatmen had taken their cargo. The big man had to shake his head. Starbin was going the long way around. And Raider had to know why. It was like an itching all over him.

He held the boat steady, considering which way to go in. Straight up the stream? Follow the bank of the creek? Find his way through the brush?

Did he feel like taking a chance?

He checked his Colt and the knife in his boot. The Winchester was still on his saddle back at the mooring. Did Regina have the good sense to hide his mount when he didn't come back? Were Starbin's men out looking for him in the night?

Somehow it didn't matter.

He felt like taking a chance.

He had to know.

But he couldn't row into the creek. The sound of the grinding oarlocks might be heard by a sentry. He decided to use one of the oars as a paddle, silently navigating the stream like an Indian in a canoe.

Between strokes, he swiped the mosquitoes away from his face. How the hell could the pesky critters see in the dark? He wished he had the same facility. He didn't see the stump sticking out of the water.

The big man froze when the bow of the boat hit the stump. The thud seemed to echo forever. It rose above the other noise from the lighted area. How the hell did they get it so bright? Something big, that was what the attorney's investigator had said.

But the echo died and the boat swung around the stump.

Raider continued slowly forward, listening to the same tinging sound he thought he had imagined earlier in the day. His heart beat a little faster, his breath seemed to catch halfway up. It didn't help when he saw the other boats parked on the bank ahead of him.

There didn't seem to be a sentry.

The noise was getting louder.

Raider pushed the oar to the bottom of the creek which was less than four feet deep. Starbin had to take his time because there was no way to handle big loads on the shallow water. He had to give the crippled man his due. The Captain had gone about his task with the persistence of a Mexican red ant rebuilding a stepped-on anthill.

The boat made a slicing sound as it ran up onto the bank. Raider got out and dragged the craft until it was secure. He turned toward the glow, the roar, listening, scanning the trees for a path. The forest was thicker along the creekbank, causing Raider to wonder if there was as much swamp on this side of the lake.

He glanced toward the other boats that rested on the bank. Probably a path there. His boots sank deep in the soft earth as he started toward the boats. Two or three of them—three when he got close enough to see. Flatboats, like the swamp people were using.

Raider found the path there. A narrow rut had been worn down between the trees. Short little deliveries, putting it together a piece at a time. There was a kind of beauty to it, even if it did seem tedious.

As soon as he turned up the path, Raider heard voices. Two men were coming straight toward him. He dove headlong between the trees, landing belly first in the mud. Something slithered out from under him without stopping to bite.

Raider felt the water seeping into his shirt. Damned swampland. The men came closer. He wondered if they would see his boat.

"I tell you, Slim, I heard somethin' out there. It was bangin' around like nobody's business."

A silence settled in for a moment.

Raider figured the man named Slim had seen his boat. What to do? If they knew he was here, maybe it was best just to jump up and take them. Commandeer one of the flatboats and get the hell away.

Someone exhaled. "Probably just that bear we been seein' around here," said the other voice—Slim no doubt. The voice took on an irritated edge. "I don't have time for this bullshit, Hargrove. We've got till the middle of the month to get ready. If we ain't, then you know what that means."

"Yes, sir."

"I'm going back to work. I suggest you stop hearing things."

"Yes, sir."

Slim tromped back up the trail into the trees.

Raider lay still, listening as Hargrove shifted around trying to get comfortable. He slapped mosquitoes for an interminable time before he dozed off. Raider was able to rise after he heard the snoring.

Slipping onto the trail, he moved slowly toward the glow that pierced the veil of the forest. When the trees opened and he gazed straight into the yellow glare, the big man decided to go back into the brush. He crouched low, crawling toward the edge of the clearing that burned bright with fire and smoke.

Some creature leaped away from the bush that Raider crawled under. He parted the vegetation enough to get a good view of things. What he saw was a little baffling.

The bright light was coming from hundreds of torches and lanterns that had been hung all over the compound. One man seemed to be doing nothing more than replenishing the flames, raising new torches and oiling the lamps. Raider watched him at work while his eyes focused.

He realized he was at eye level with railroad tracks. A stony bed of gravel rose up to support two train cars that sat on the track. The engine was new and shiny, like it had never done service on a main line. Behind it sat a black, sinister looking boxcar. Men were hard at work on the car, nailing strange looking squares of iron and wood to the body.

Raider was able to make out the dark-eyed slits between the strange squares. They were spaced just far enough apart for a man to stand every three feet with a rifle. Eleven or twelve slits at shoulder height.

The work went on feverishly. What was it the man in the darkness had said? *Get this thing ready by the middle of the month.* By the fifteenth, Raider thought. That was when it was going to happen. At least now he knew that the plot wasn't a lie.

He froze when something rustled in the woods behind him. Tromping and sloshing echoed in the trees. Maybe it was the bear. A steam whistle screeched from the train, drowning out the noise. It seemed to scare whatever it was, because the thing moved away from him.

Raider turned back to the fury of the work that went on in the glowing compound. He had two choices. He could lie there until things got quiet and then poke around on the sly. Or he could walk straight into the camp, introduce himself as one of Starbin's men and see if they would show him around.

A man passed by him with a crate of dynamite. It was one of the same crates he had seen on the dock behind Starbin's place. These boys were serious, he thought. But they sure weren't in any position to take over the state of Texas. And Starbin hadn't transported that steam locomotive and boxcar across the black lake. Those tracks had been set down specially for the train. Maybe it had come from Louisiana. They couldn't be that far from the border.

He had to get a better look. Maybe if he just waltzed out of the woods. . . . There were enough men around that he might get lost in the fray. There had to be a way to . . .

A rifle hammer clicked under a thumb.

Raider was turning up as cold iron pressed against his cheek.

"Don't move, boy. Hey, Slim. I got a . . ."

The rifleman's face had lifted into the light.

Raider decided to disobey him and move.

He grabbed the barrel of the rifle, immediately shoving it down into the soft earth. The man's finger tripped the trigger, only the rifle didn't explode on the business end. Instead, it blew up in the man's face.

The man fell backward, holding his eyes.

Raider jumped up, starting into the compound. The chortling of rifle levers turned him back into the swamp. He wheeled and ran as fast as he could in the mire.

Winchesters exploded from the bright light. Slugs whizzed past the big man who tried to keep a straight line. He didn't want to duck into the path of a bullet.

He knew he was going deeper into the swamp.

His legs struck cool, knee-deep water that suddenly spread

out around him. At least the earth was firm beneath the pool. Sometimes it worked like that. Then sometimes it didn't. He tried to remember if there was any quicksand in east Texas.

He reached the deepest part of the water, stepping off into a deep hole. His boots groped for purchase as he fought to get back into the shallows. For a moment he thought he might not make it, but then he felt something under his boot heel. He thrashed his arms, propelling himself upward.

The water swirled around his knees again. Only this time he was wet from head to foot. His hat had floated off somewhere. And his Peacemaker was waterlogged. He drew the piece, shaking out some of the water. It might work if he needed it. He holstered the weapon, thinking the first thing he needed was to get the hell out of the dark swamp.

Something sloshed again in the bog. A dull grunt followed with another echo. Then a bear roared. Maybe it was the old bear the men had been talking about. Raider didn't fear it as much anymore. He had other things to worry him. He startled wading again, wondering if the men would follow.

At first it seemed as though they were going to let him get away.

He trudged through the morass for a long time without hearing a thing.

Then the echo of the baying hounds filtered through the trees and Raider figured they were not going to stop until they had him in chains.

He ran on through the night, trying every trick he knew. At one point, the trees were close enough for him to climb and go from tree to tree until he had put a gap in the trail scent. But that didn't seem to help. The baying got louder.

Raider tried to take them away from the direction of his boat. Or at least as near as he could determine direction in the dark. If he lost the dogs, he might be able to double back along the shore of the lake until he found some sort of vessel. Then he had to get across the dark water again, back to his mount. Ride straight for Beaumont and send wires to Austin and to Chicago. Raise a militia. What if nobody believed him? Hell, he still wasn't sure what the men in the compound were up to, let alone whether they intended to cause trouble. That could wait though, until he was out of the swamp.

The yelping hounds were closer now. Raider had always heard that bloodhounds couldn't track over water, but that wasn't proving to be true. He wished he had some pepper to sprinkle in his path. But he didn't have pepper, so he just ran on.

He was looking back over his shoulder when he heard the grunt ahead of him. Wheeling around, he stared straight at a pair of glowing eyes. A heavy-footed animal sloshed in the water. The goddamned bear.

Raider drew his Colt, thinking his only chance was a lucky shot to the bear's eye. Even at close range the slug wouldn't penetrate a bear's skull. Not even an old bear at the end of his life.

The bear moved forward, snorting, not ten yards away from the big man.

Raider held still against a tree. Something crawled over his shoulder and splashed into the swamp. The bear walked past him, sniffing the air. Suddenly he growled and startled running in the opposite direction. The smell of a human had startled him. He knew that smell was danger, the same way that Raider knew the baying of the hounds was trouble.

He started forward again, tired but unable to give up as long as he had any strength left in his body.

He was still moving when the sun started to spread a purple haze over the tops of the swamp trees.

The dogs were on the run but they didn't seem to be as close as they had been.

Raider stopped for a while, listening as the barking became a faint echo. He took a deep breath and smiled as he let it out. The bear had saved him. The dogs had picked up its scent and were on its trail. Now all he had to do was get back to the lake. But hell, how would that help? He couldn't retrieve his boat now that they knew about him. He'd have to find another way across the water.

He laughed defeatedly at himself.

He was already making plans and he wasn't even out of the swamp yet.

Turning in the cold water, he started forward again, scattering the alligators and water snakes in his way.

CHAPTER SEVENTEEN

Raider pushed out of the swamp into the orange shimmer of an east Texas sunrise over the lake. Did the sun seem brighter in the east, or was it a hallucination brought on by the horrible night in the bog? Raider didn't have time to strip his clothes and wash them. He did stop to pick off a few leeches that had a hold on him.

Something told him to turn to his left, away from the dogs. He could still hear them, a faint noise in the cool morning air. He felt a sick rumbling in his gut. He turned it away with the sheer force of will.

Tired, hungry, aching for sleep.

But there was no quit in him.

Maybe there was a way to get south from this end of the lake.

He continued along the lakefront until he came on a brown shanty that seemed to be crumbling into the water.

Raider held still, listening for signs of life. There were two old rowboats resting next to the shanty. He wondered if they would hold water. Best to draw his Colt.

Cautiously, the big man stepped up to the dilapidated door of the shack. The door fell off the hinges when he pulled it open. Someone gasped inside the moldy hovel. Raider thumbed the hammer of the gun.

"Please, don't kill me, mister."

Raider squinted in the shadows. "I ain't gonna kill you."

"Steal anything I got," the man whined. "But don't take my life."

Raider waved the barrel of the Colt. "Come on out here where I can see you, boy."

The man trembled as he stepped into the first light of morning. He was a toothless old swamp rat. Probably the kind of man who hated company and just wanted to be alone. Raider wished the old man had made better use of the water that cried out to be bathed in.

"What's your name, pardner?"

The man seemed baffled by the question but managed to squeak out, "Gus."

"Okay, Gus, I need a boat. You got two of 'em."

"Take one," the old man replied. "Steal it outright. I only use one and they both float. Ain't mine anyway. I just took up here. Livin' on catfish and turtles. Go on, take one."

Raider reached into his wet pocket, wondering if he had anything to offer the old coot. To his surprise, he came up with a twenty dollar gold piece. He flashed the double eagle in the morning sun.

"Twenty dollars," he said. "For a boat that doesn't take on water."

The sparkle of gold seemed to calm the swamp rat's nerves. "Hell, you can have 'em both for twenty dollars. Take the one on the left. It don't have no leaks."

Raider nodded and turned to gaze out over the smooth water. "I need to get to Beaumont, old timer. Which way should I go?"

Gus rubbed his grizzled chin, cogitating. "Well, you could row south. But you're gonna be on the water a long time. 'Course, if'n you make it all the way to the Sabine, you'll have easy goin'. But that's a long way off. Nope, best to row back across the lake and pick up a horse in Zavalla."

Raider exhaled. He would have given a month's pay for a warm bath, food, and enough sleep to straighten out his head. He flipped the double eagle to the swamp rat and asked for help in launching the rowboat.

"Good luck, stranger," Gus called as the big man rowed away.

Raider dug into the oars, rowing until the pain got too great. Then he rested a while, picking up when the burn went away from his muscles. He intended to go back to Starbin's place, if he could find it. Then he could steal a horse. Or maybe Regina had left his black by the dock. If he got lucky, he might be able to arrest Starbin. After all, the captain only had five men backing him up. Raider had taken care of more men at one clip. Use some dynamite from the crates on Starbin's dock.

But as it turned out, nothing happened at all like he hoped it would.

Still, he thought he got a break when he reached the other side of the lake. After searching most of the morning for the creek that led back to Starbin's dock, he saw the boatmen entering the lake from between the trees. Raider watched them lapping across the water at a surprising clip. He felt exhausted after starting up three different streams that were dead ends. But he could not stop now. If he found a horse and got away from Starbin, then he might make camp and sleep for a couple of hours.

When the boatmen were out of sight, he strained at the oars again, steering the wooden craft up into the creek. The going was slower against the current, but he had the dock in sight before too long. The bow of the vessel bumped against the mooring with a loud thud.

Raider looked up, wondering if Regina was on duty. Nothing. The pile of munitions was still covered with the tarp.

He crawled out of the boat, standing up on shaky legs. He needed to rest. Everything was starting to look fuzzy.

Maybe he could crawl under the tarp and go to sleep. Regina might show up. Then again, Starbin's men might be looking for him after he didn't return last night. He wheeled when he heard the horse snorting.

His body came back to life.

The stallion whinnied in the bushes.

Raider raced to the mount, untying the reins from the tree limb. Regina had done well. Maybe he could slip away without anyone seeing him. Of course, his rifle would come in handy if . . . he touched the sling ring but there was nothing there. Maybe Regina had taken his Winchester to shoot a water moccasin or to scare off an alligator.

Something rattled behind him.

Raider wheeled toward the sound, dropping his hand toward the redwood handle of his Colt.

"That won't be necessary," someone said.

Raider hesitated. Where had he heard that voice before? The man was back in the trees, hiding.

"Take your gun out of the holster with your left hand," the

voice said. "Slowly. Then drop it on the ground."

Raider knew that a rifle—probably his own—was pointed at him. He obeyed the command, trying not to tremble. "It's me. Buck. I got lost out there when I was gator huntin'."

The bushes parted and a well-dressed gentleman showed himself in the dim forest light. "A man doesn't go hunting alligators without his rifle."

Raider suddenly remembered the voice. "Holt, is that you?"

"None other," Peter Holt replied. "Sorry I couldn't get here faster."

Holt lowered the rifle and stepped forward a little.

Raider shook his head. "Boy, am I glad t' see you. You wouldn't b'lieve what's goin' on t'other side o' this lake."

"I might," Holt replied coolly.

The big man started to bend down for his gun. "Let me get my iron and I'll tell you what I've learned so . . ."

Holt raised Raider's Winchester again. "I can't let you do that, Raider." The dapper politician was frowning now.

"So that's how it is," Raider said, his eyes narrowing. "But you helped me back in Austin."

"Did I?"

The big man scowled at Holt. "S'pose you tell me what's goin' on, boy."

Holt snapped his fingers. Suddenly Baker was there, tying Raider's hands behind his back. He didn't have enough strength to resist.

"You almost had us fooled, big 'un," Bake said. "Good thing Major Holt here straightened us out."

"I still don't get it," Raider offered.

Bake slapped him on the shoulder. "Don't worry, pardner. You will."

They took him back to the house, locking him in the dismal cellar, chaining his hands and feet together with manacles.

Holt stood over him, smiling with a calm expression. "Mr. Raider, you are the luckiest son of a bitch alive."

Raider chortled disgustedly, lifting his chained hands. "How you figure that, Holt?"

The gentleman took a seat on a round wooden keg, like he had been waiting all along for this confrontation. "Let's start at the beginning. Do you have any thoughts on the subject?"

Raider could barely see his face in the dim basement. "Well," the big man drawled, "I'm bettin' you ain't from the office of the state attorney."

"Precisely," Holt replied. "You see, I wasn't working for Forbin at all. In fact, it was my men who killed him."

"And you was comin' back to Forbin's place t' pick up the evidence 'gainst you," Raider offered.

Holt nodded appreciatively. "But you see, there was no way for you to know that. And when I talked you into running away, your luck held up for a long time."

Raider leaned back against the stone cellar wall. "That wanted poster that turned up. You did it?"

Holt smiled. "No, that wasn't me. The territorial authorities came up with that. No, you see, that's where I knew you were lucky. I was detained in Austin after I let you go."

"Why'd you free me in the first place?" the big man asked. "Why didn't you have your boys just take care o' me? Shoot me in the back?"

"You were more useful to me on the run," Holt replied. "If you had turned up dead, the local authorities would have searched for an explanation. They would have learned that you were sent to work with Forbin. Instead, they thought you were the killer."

Raider laughed. "And you said I was lucky."

"Oh, you were. You managed to get to Beaumont and meet Fernandez. Then you made it all the way to Zavalla without being apprehended. I was amazed when I met Captain Starbin in Zavalla. When he described you to me, I couldn't believe it at first."

Raider shook his head. "I still don't get it. Why didn't you just send a message to Starbin? Tell him I was comin' this way?"

"I intended to," Holt replied. "But as I said, I was detained. You see, one of Forbin's neighbors thought he saw me going into Forbin's house the night that I met you there. One of the local constables recognized me and hauled me in for questioning. But you see, I had already arranged an alibi. A certain bevy of young ladies swore that I had been with them all night."

"What'd you pay them?"

"Handsome wages," Holt said. "But it was worth it. Of course, the sheriff didn't buy my story for a moment. I had

Texas Rangers and deputies on my tail from then on. I couldn't even send a wire or a letter. Naturally, I had to come here in person. By then, you had already infiltrated the camp."

"Huh. I reckon I did."

Holt stood up. "A pity that you can't really be on our side. Your luck has run out. We could use a man like you, but I know you won't relent."

Raider wasn't sure what it meant to relent, but he knew he didn't want to do it. "Funny how things fell a certain way," he said. "Mebbe the Rangers followed you here, Holt."

The dapper outlaw shrugged. "We aren't doing anything wrong."

"What about that pile o' stolen stuff in the swamp? And that lookout on the other side o' the lake?"

"The stolen goods on this side will be destroyed soon," Holt replied. "And as for the other side . . . well, can't you figure that out?"

Raider didn't want him to go just yet so he played it to the end. "You brought that train in, didn't you? Laid that track. And you're armoring the boxcar. It's all part o' the same plan. You're trainin' these men t' hit hard. One group on horseback, the other from the boxcar."

Holt shook his head. "Tsk. Smart, strong, and lucky. You are quite a man, Raider. You managed to find our little factory."

"December fifteenth," the big man went on. "You're gonna kill somebody. But who?"

"That I can't tell you."

"What diff'rence does it make, Holt? You're gonna kill me anyway. I'm s'prised you ain't done it already."

Holt shrugged. "You'd be dead if it was up to me. But you see, our mad Captain has other plans for you. Especially after you diddled his wife. He isn't at all happy about that."

"So tell me. What are you up to?"

Holt sighed. "Oh, I suppose I'd tell you if I wasn't a superstitious man. But I don't want to jinx it."

"Who's b'hind this?" Raider asked.

"Starbin, of course."

Raider scoffed at the gentleman. "He ain't the brains here. You might be usin' him t' get you some things you need.

Stirrin' it all up in Texas when your real target is in Louisiana."

"You *have* been busy," Holt replied.

"Ever been to Shreveport, Petey?"

Holt waved him off. "You still don't know our true plan, otherwise you wouldn't be asking."

"I know this," the big man challenged. "Starbin's South ain't gonna rise again. You may have convinced him so he'd throw in with you, but the Confederacy is dead an' buried."

"Don't you think I'm aware of that?" Holt replied. "But when all of this is over, the finger will be pointing at Starbin. And our interests will be served a hundred times over while we get away scot-free."

Raider glared up at him. "We? Who you workin' for, Holt? You didn't get that train rig for free. Has this got somethin' t' do with the railroad?"

Holt grinned from ear to ear. "'The evil lives on after men,' Raider. Shakespeare said that. And believe me, when we're finished, this evil will live on for a long time."

"You better kill me, Holt. If I get free, I'm gonna hurt you good."

"You won't get free, you Pinkerton ape. Like I said, your luck has run out."

Holt turned and left with Raider cursing him all the way.

When he was gone, the big man leaned back again, wondering about the state of his fortune.

Maybe Holt had been right, maybe his luck was all gone. It really didn't seem that important at this sorry point. Perhaps things would look different after he had slept for a while.

He closed his eyes and slipped into an aching, fitful slumber.

Raider startled and tried to sit up when the door creaked open. He expected Holt again, the traitor, the man who was going to kill him. But instead of the dapper villain, he got a whiff of an all too familiar perfume.

"Regina?"

She eased the door shut and put a finger to her lips. Sidling closer to the big man, she touched his face with a cool cloth. "Don't talk too loud," she whispered. "I don't want Bond to find out I'm down here."

"How the hell did you get past the guard?"

She shrugged slightly. “Baker? I had to promise him something.”

“What?”

“This.”

She pressed her lips to his, darting her tongue between his lips.

Raider drew back a little. “Sorry, honey, it’s too late for that. You can see I ain’t in no shape t’ play ’round with you.”

That didn’t seem to discourage her. “I brought you food.”

Regina unfolded a napkin with meat and bread inside it. She hand-fed him and then offered him water from a metal dipper. Raider wondered if it was going to be his last meal.

“What time is it?” he asked.

“After midnight. I heard the clock strike one on the way down here. How are you feeling?”

He chortled defeatedly. “Not so good. I ache all over an’ my head feels like somebody split it with a poleax.”

She started to daub his forehead with the cool cloth. “I’m so sorry, Raider. I never wanted it to be like this. You should have gone for help right away. If you had . . .”

“Shoulda, coulda, woulda,” the big man replied. “If the dog hadn’t stopped t’ lift ’is leg, he woulda caught the rabbit.”

She tried to laugh at his joke but her heart seemed to be sinking as fast as his. “You saw Holt,” she offered.

Raider nodded. “He hornswoggled me in Austin. Convinced me he was workin’ with the man who was investigatin’ your hubby.” He gazed into her eyes. “Hey, did ol’ Bond figger out that you showed me where the boats were landin’?”

“No. Not yet. When he asked where you were, I said I hadn’t seen you. I guess he believed me.”

Raider frowned. “Holt said Bond knew ’bout you an’ me . . . you know, in the bunkhouse.”

“Bond hasn’t said anything to me,” Regina replied.

“Huh. Holt was probably just guessin’. Either that, or he’s plannin’ t’ convince your husband that we did.”

Her hand began to rub the cool cloth over his chest. “I want to again. Right here.”

Raider lifted his chained wrists. “How?”

“Like this.”

She started on the buttons of his jeans. Raider wanted to resist, at least until he realized that he was growing hard.

Then he told himself that it didn't matter. Hell, it might be his last time anyway.

Regina had begun to breathe erratically. She jerked his manhood as she hiked up her gown. Raider watched as she straddled his crotch. Her hand guided him to the moist font of her cunt.

She grunted, trying to take him in. But the angle was awkward so she had to shift her body again. Finally he felt the tightness of her pussy as she impaled herself on his prick.

"It's good," she whispered, "even like this."

The big man could not argue. He leaned back against the wall, trying to pretend he was in a fancy whorehouse. Regina stopped for a moment, sitting on his lap with his cock inside her. She freed her breasts from the constraints of her undergarments, pushing her chest into his face.

Raider licked her nipples as she resumed her motion.

He tried to help her a little by bouncing off the floor. But it was no use. He was chained and there was nothing he could do about it.

Regina didn't seem to care. "So big," she groaned. "Feels so good inside me."

He felt himself rising. His cock expanded inside her as he burst forth. Regina trembled when he came. She pressed her mouth against his, kissing him like a new bride.

"I love you, Raider."

He stroked her red hair. "I love you, too, honey."

Did it really matter that he didn't mean it? She probably didn't mean it either. But it made them both feel good to say it.

Regina rolled off him, sitting beside him. "Look, I've got you all wet. I better clean you up."

She used the cloth to mop her thick moistness from his crotch.

Somehow the whole thing gave Raider a sense of satisfaction. Maybe Bond Starbin was mounting some sort of crazy offensive in Louisiana, but Raider was downstairs giving his wife something Starbin didn't have. The thought and Regina's attentive hand brought his prick back to life.

"You want it again?" he asked her.

She nodded. "Let me sit on it."

"No. Here, I can turn a little. Mebbe like this."

He managed to turn sideways. Regina was right there,

sliding over to him. She wrapped her leg over his hip, once again guiding his cock between her legs.

"Hard," she whispered. "Fuck me as hard as you can."

A sweat broke out over their bodies as they ground together in the musty cellar. Regina bit her lip, quaking as she found one release after another. Raider wished he could get on top of her, but the chains kept them in the awkward position. Still, he managed to work up enough friction to trigger his second release.

Regina shivered, locking her legs around him. "Don't pull out yet. Leave it in there. Please."

"Honey, maybe you oughta be gettin' back upstairs."

She shook her head. "No. I want to stay with you. If I leave, Baker is going to want what I promised him. And I can't stand the thought of him touching me. I only want you, Raider. I want you to take me away from here."

"Right. You think you can unlock these chains and get me a gun?"

"I can try," she offered. "I've been thinking on it . . . if I could get a hacksaw, I could . . . oh my God!"

They heard the heavy footsteps on the stairs to the cellar.

Regina tried to get up, but the door swung open before she could disengage herself.

Peter Holt came through the door first, followed by Baker who was carrying the legless Starbin.

Holt pointed at the couple on the dirt floor of the basement. "You see, Bond. I told you the truth. Look at them. Like two rutting pigs."

Regina sat up, straightening herself, covering her bosom.

Raider just lay there, smiling. "Yeah, she needed it pretty good, Bond. An' I took care o' her. Don't thank me for doin' your husbandly duty. It was all my pleasure."

Baker scowled at the big man. "You want me to cut his dick off, Captain Starbin?"

The captain was glaring maniacally at the man on the floor. "No. I have something else in mind."

"Do your worst," Raider replied. "You may kill me, but there'll be somebody t' take my place. You'll see."

Holt was grinning, satisfied with himself. "Hollow words. By the time we're finished, it will be too late."

Raider tried to make his laughter convincing. "Yeah? Shit

on both o' you. The South ain't gonna rise again, Starbin. You hear me? Holt here is just usin' you."

"Silence!" Starbin cried. "Private Baker, take me upstairs. Holt, you bring my wife."

"No!" Regina cried. "I want to stay with Raider. I love him, not you. I'll die with him if I have to."

Bond Starbin turned his gaze on his lovely wife. "Oh, don't worry, my dear. You'll die with him, like the whore of Babylon that you are. But first, I want my men to have their use of you. If you want to be a harlot, then you shall get your wish. Bring her."

Holt grabbed Regina and started to drag her out.

Raider spat at the dapper outlaw. "You better kneel t'night an' pray to God that I don't get loose, Holt. If I get my hands on you . . ."

"Hollow words," Holt repeated. "Besides, the only one who's going to be kneeling tonight will be the little lady here. And I think she'll begin with me."

Raider pulled at his chains, shouting his rage. He cursed them until the door closed. Then he cursed them some more. He screamed until his voice went raw. Then he leaned back, wondering if there was some way to get the hell out of this awful mess.

CHAPTER EIGHTEEN

Raider had never cared much for waiting under any circumstances, much less waiting in a dank, dark cellar. His mind seemed to be working overtime, as if the dimness and the musty smell drove him to thinking. A lot of damned thinking. Too damned much.

Second-guessing was always easier after things fell apart. Raider had arrived at the conclusion that his biggest fault had to be his tendency to rush into something like a bull after a trespasser in his meadow. But when did he get a chance to stop and take a tally? Doc Weatherbee, his old partner, had always been the calm one. Just ease up, figure it with logic. Raider's logic always seemed to come too late.

The big man wouldn't have minded having his old partner back. Or so he decided on his fifth day of captivity. December seventh. He had figured the date with scratch marks on the stone basement wall, using his manacles to etch the deep scrawls. Yep, Doc would have looked pretty good right now. If he had been anywhere close by, he would have been searching for Raider. At least there'd be an outside chance.

Raider thought a lot about the way Doc had gone and married that girl. No partner after that. Raider just couldn't stand to see the new partners die. That nimble-footed Weatherbee, the Harvard dandy, had always been able to get out of the way. It was kind of a pity that he hadn't been able to get out of the way of that girl.

Raider had *chosen* to work alone. It was his own fault that nobody out there gave two damns about his disappearance. If he was going to get out of this, he had to do it by himself.

• • •

Raider counted the scratches on the wall. Seven of them. December ninth. The day went the same as the rest of them. Waking to the rooster as it cried from the barnyard. Making his mark on the wall. By then Baker arrived with his breakfast, a big meal of pancakes, bacon, eggs, grits, and ham.

"You're feedin' me good," Raider said.

Baker shrugged. "Yeah, I reckon."

"Why?"

A smile from the outlaw. "Oh, I don't know. I reckon he wants you healthy so when you die it'll take a long time. I figure he has a plan to drag it out, so you'll suffer a lot."

"I'm eatin'," the big man replied. *So I'll be strong*, he thought. *So I'll be able to make my move when the chance comes*. "An' it'll come."

Baker glared at him. "What'd you say?"

Raider shoved a pancake into his mouth.

Baker watched him. The outlaw had been trying to draw Raider out for a whole week. All he usually got were grunts and groans, so Raider's question about the food got him started again.

"You want to know about your lady?" Baker asked.

Raider lifted his black eyes. "Keep your mouth shut, boy."

"Whatta you gonna do, break them chains and beat me to death?" Baker laughed. "Shit, cowboy. Your tit's in the ringer. So is Miss Regina's. And she's got some big ones."

Raider threw the plate at him. Grits and long syrup splashed in Baker's gloating face. He wiped the hot food away, yowling like a hurt pup.

When Baker had recovered a little, he immediately drew his gun. "I oughta blow your brains out."

"Go ahead," the big man challenged. "You'd be doin' me a favor. Only I pity your ass when another Pink catches up t' you."

Baker smirked and holstered the weapon. "Ain't nobody catchin' up to us, big 'un. And you're gonna die soon enough. And it's gonna be slow. You know, we been havin' a good time with Miss Regina. Just like you did."

"Bastard."

Baker wheeled and left in a hurry.

Raider sat there all day, thinking, trying to move as much as he could in his chains. He didn't want his arms and legs to tighten up. He had to be fresh when his chance came. And it would come. He had to believe that.

At the end of the aimless day, one of the other hands brought his dinner. Raider ate again, wanting to keep his strength. The man just stood there and watched him, as if he was some animal in a zoo.

"What're you lookin' at?" Raider challenged.

The man shrugged. "Just wondered what a Pinkerton looked like. I kinda wanted to be a Pink before I fell in with these boys."

Raider's eyes opened a little wider. "You get me outta here, son, an' I'll see to it you have a fair trial. Then mebbe, after you . . ."

"Don't soap me," the man replied. "I know a man's been a outlaw can't be a Pink. And these boys is outside the law."

"You ain't?"

"For now," the man replied. "But after I make me a whole lot of money, I aim to go back to Mississippi and start me up a farm."

"No shortcuts, boy. Throw in with me. I'll see to it . . ."

The man drew his pistol. "Eat."

Raider picked up a chicken leg. "How are they treatin' the woman?"

"Ever'body's had a turn. 'Ceptin' Baker. He don't want none of it. I think maybe he don't like women too much."

Raider bit into the chicken, which was tough.

He finished his dinner and tried to sleep.

The next morning, when the rooster didn't wake him, he knew that the tough old bird had been his dinner the night before. Starbin had killed his rooster, a sign that he was pulling out soon and not coming back.

"December tenth," he said as he marked the day on the wall.

They'd be coming for him soon. If their strike happened on the fifteenth, and if Starbin didn't plan on returning to east Texas, then they'd have to get rid of Raider pretty soon. When he heard the footsteps on the stairs, he wondered if maybe this morning was his last on earth.

"Breakfast," Baker said, smiling. "Sorry I didn't bring your dinner last night, but I was busy with Miss Regina."

"Sure you were," the big man scoffed, taking the plate into his hands.

"Not gonna throw it at me?" Baker asked.

Raider bit into the ham, ignoring the outlaw. He knew that his chance was coming soon. Probably on the eleventh or the twelfth. If they killed the rooster, they'd be pulling out soon.

And he was right. That night, instead of dinner, they came and unlocked his chains. Four of them, in white robes with guns drawn. They marched him out of the basement and up the stairs. Raider's legs felt wobbly, but he still tried to move.

When he swung at Baker, the outlaw simply raised a rifle butt and clapped Raider on the jaw.

The big man went down, blacking out.

When he woke up, the woman was beside him and they were both in a hell of a lot of trouble.

Starbin had crucified them.

Raider and the woman had been raised on two huge crosses of wood. Their wrists and ankles had been bound by wire. Raider glanced over at Regina who looked dead already. She was completely naked and limp.

The big man's black eyes rolled in a circle. He saw his captors huddled around the crosses in white robes. Klansmen. He had seen it before. Why couldn't some men just admit that the South had been beaten?

Torches lit the yard in the dim light of dusk.

Raider tried to look down at his feet, where two men were stacking cordwood. He counted the number of men at work. Fifteen in all. Some of the others had come across the lake, either that or they were new recruits.

Captain Starbin and his father were there, both dressed in their white robes. Raider wondered if he might be dreaming. When one of the men laid a whip across his belly, he knew he was awake.

Captain Starbin motioned from his wheelchair. "That's enough, Baker."

Raider's eyes were blurry. He squinted, trying to make out the faces of his tormenters. What difference did it make? He was going to be dead soon. Still, he just wanted to see them, if for no other reason than the fact that he might recognize them in Hell.

"Aw, heck, Captain," Baker said. "You never let me use my whip."

"I want him strong," Starbin replied. "I don't want him to

die until he realizes how painful it has been for him."

Raider tried to spit but his mouth was dry.

He felt something hitting his feet. They were stacking the wood higher. What the hell did Starbin have in mind? Raider glared down at him from the cross, scowling defiantly even at the end.

"Yes," Starbin replied. "I'm going to burn you at the stake. And these crosses will burn as well. I want them to be a symbol for anyone who comes along. Southern gentlemen will no longer tolerate the ways of nigger-loving Yankee scum. Do you hear me, Pinkerton?"

Raider cleared his throat, managing to cough up a hocker that he launched in Starbin's general direction.

"You'll have to do better than that," the captain said. "Look at him, Peter. A beaten man."

Holt was there beside the captain, although he was the only one not wearing a white robe. "How the mighty are fallen," Holt said. "This form of demise was a wonderful idea, Captain Starbin."

Old man Starbin cheered, giving his version of a rebel yell. "Yee-hah."

"After the great day, we shall be strong," Captain Starbin intoned. "No more Yankee carpetbaggers to steal our fortunes and rape our women."

"Whatta you know about women?" Raider cried. "Look at what you done to your wife."

"She was unfaithful to me!"

"What choice did you give 'er?"

Starbin waved toward Baker.

Baker laid the whip across Raider's stomach again.

The big man held his tongue. He didn't want to cry out, to show Starbin that he was hurting. Instead, he tried to spit again.

"A futile gesture," Peter Holt said. "And all the more fitting when you consider what we have in mind for you. Can you figure it out, Mr. Pinkerton? Look above you."

Raider lifted his eyes to see men stringing oil lanterns over him in the trees. They were attached to some sort of mechanical device. He gazed back down at the pile of wood that had grown beneath him.

"You see," Holt went on, "as the lanterns are set into motion, they'll drop inch by inch until they hit the piles of wood.

Or the cross. They they'll burst open and the oil will spread as will the flame. And don't think for a moment that it won't work. That's why we're rigging four lanterns."

Raider tried to laugh. "Can't just kill me outright, huh? Don't have the guts for it. That's what I hate about your kind, Holt. You're good at figurin' an' weaselin' around. But when it comes t' lookin' a man in the eye and facin' 'im down, you ain't got what it takes. You couldn't stand toe to toe with somebody who had a fair chance."

"Perhaps not," Holt said. "But that isn't really the point here, is it? No, I'd say you're the one who will never again stand toe to toe with anyone."

Holt picked up a piece of kindling and dropped it on the pile.

Raider glared at him, never taking his eyes off the dapper man. "Go on an' tell me, Holt. What is it you boys got cooked up in Shreveport? You can tell me. I ain't goin' nowhere."

"Like I told you before," Holt replied. "I don't want to jinx it. Have a hot time, Raider. Get it? Hot time."

He erupted with a crazy howling.

Captain Starbin poked Holt with a stick. "That's enough, Holt. You don't want the others to see that you're having a good time. I don't want the spirit of mirth to rule our task."

Holt bristled for a moment but finally simmered down. "Yes, *sir*, Captain Starbin! At your command, *sir*!"

Starbin shot him a dirty look and then went back to supervising Raider's funeral pyre.

The big man felt the pain in his arms. He tried to move but there was no way to get free. This was it. The final showdown. And he wasn't even going out with a gun in his hand. All a man could ask at the end was a fighting chance and he wasn't even getting that.

The robed men continued until total darkness fell over the grounds of the Starbin mansion. Raider wondered if the captain planned to torch his own house. Maybe this was Starbin's way of getting rid of his old identity, to throw the law off his trail after he had done his heinous deed.

"You won't make it!" Raider cried. "You hear me! Somebody will stop you somehow. They'll stop you dead!"

"You won't be stopping anybody," Starbin cried. "You, a son of Dixie. How could you not throw in with us?"

"I'm born an' bred in Dixie," Raider cried. "But I never

hated any colored man because his skin was differ'nt than mine. An' I never hated no Yankee less'n he done me wrong. I can tell you this, too, Starbin. Lookin' at you, I'm glad the South lost the war. If I had to put up with . . . oof . . ."

The whip had bit him again. He wanted to yell some more but he realized that it was too late. One of the men had lit the lanterns and set them to swinging on their lines. Raider could hear the clicking mechanism as the lamps began their slow, inevitable descent.

Starbin's men started to mobilize and move out.

The captain and his father were helped onto a wagon. Raider wondered how they were going to get across the lake to the train. They probably had five or six longboats waiting. Maybe even a dozen. Raider shook his head, amazed that he would think of such things so close to death.

Holt was the last one to stare up at him from the ground. "Anything you want to say to me, Pinkerton?"

Raider spoke through clenched teeth. "You can kiss my ass in Hell!"

Holt had another good laugh as he walked away.

Raider listened for a long time until the last echoes of their departure had disappeared in the still, night air. It was a pretty evening, just cool enough to make it brisk without being uncomfortable. Raider lifted his eyes to the lanterns as they winched down.

Maybe a rain would come.

Sky too clear.

Maybe a wind would blow out the lanterns.

Not even the slightest breeze to stir the leaves.

The mechanism clicked with maddening precision.

"Son of a bitch."

He looked over at Regina, who was lucky enough to be unconscious.

His eyes lifted to heaven. "Well, Old Boy, I ain't gonna ask You for nothin'. Just get me to Hell as quick as You can."

The first lantern hit the top of the cross that Regina had been tied on. It broke, sending oil down to the pile of wood. No flame though. Maybe it wouldn't work. Maybe Starbin had been . . .

A second lantern burst and the fire spread down the line of oil.

The kindling caught with ease.

Raider felt the heat rising almost immediately.

His head began to spin, his eyes went dry.

The flames licked the bottoms of his boots.

This was it. The last ride. One more way to die. Only this time he was really heading for Hell.

He looked up through the wavy lines of heat.

Lucifer had come to take him. He saw the shape moving toward his pyre. No, it wasn't Old Pitch himself, but one of his minions climbed out of the fiery pit of sulphur and brimstone.

The demon seemed to be fanning the fire.

Raider looked down before he passed out. He recognized the face of Lucifer's sidekick. Was it really him?

His last thought before he lost consciousness was to wonder how in God's name Henry Stokes had beat him to Hell.

The cold water stung his face.

Raider opened his eyes to the bright glare of the sun overhead. At first the big man thought it was the light of God Himself. He had heard stories about seeing the light, about the dead passing over into it.

Then the face of Henry Stokes loomed between Raider and the light.

Raider sat up, causing Stokes to jump back.

"Damn," Stokes said, "I figured that water'd set you to movin'. Wasn't sure how much longer you'd sleep."

Every pore of Raider's body ached. His feet felt tender. Stokes had taken his boots off. He was lying in the front yard of some run-down mansion.

"Where the hell am I?" he asked the short man in the black derby.

Stokes chewed on a sprig of sassafras root. "Reckon you're in Texas, Raider. Near Zavalla, same as me. Had a devil of a time findin' you, least ways till I hit Beaumont. That Fernandez feller was helpful. How'd you get on to him anyway?"

It all came rushing back to him. Starbin and his men had left to go across the lake. That train was waiting to take them to their rendezvous. Who the hell were they going to kill?

"You know you got a price on your head?" Stokes offered.

Raider scowled at his associate. "Well, I reckon I oughta thank you for savin' my fool neck."

Stokes shook it off. "No, you don't have to. I'm just sorry I didn't get to you sooner. Got a couple of sorry blisters on your soles."

"I'll pop 'em and wrap my feet," the big man replied. "Use lard to oil up the burns."

"The woman was luckier," Stokes said. "Good thing the agency sent me to find you."

Raider tried to get to his feet but the blisters were tender. "Where is she?"

"In the house. I put her to bed. She's pretty worn. I did get her to eat this mornin'. Looks like somebody's been treatin' her pretty bad."

"More like ever'body treatin' 'er bad."

"Sorry. Been watchin' this place since yesterday. Figured I had to move when they fired you up."

Raider sat on the grass, wishing his feet would stop hurting.

He told Stokes about Starbin's little army. About the train on the other side of the lake. The way Starbin had been shipping the stolen munitions little by little to the train. He kept saying that he wished he knew what the hell they were up to. It all had something to do with Starbin's dream of the Confederacy rising again.

Stokes frowned, sighing, looking away.

Now Raider had never worked much with the paunchy man from Georgia, but he knew a mood when he saw one. "You know somethin', don't you, Stokes."

Henry tipped back his derby and nodded. "Maybe I do. Here, look at this."

Stokes pulled a flyer out of his duster pocket and handed it to Raider.

It read: "Appearing for one hour only, President Rutherford B. Hayes, To Speak on Reconstruction and other matters. Public Landing, Shreveport, Louisiana. December 15." A likeness of the bearded president rested in the middle of the writing.

"Goddamn them," Raider said. "They're gonna kill the president."

Stokes sighed calmly. "Yeah, it looks that way."

Raider began to describe the boxcar. He told about the snake-eyed slits on the sides, where the rifles would be. He mentioned the dynamite he had seen. Fifteen or twenty men at least.

"And we practiced too," he went on. "Ridin' down on a man and shootin' 'im in the heart. They're gonna hit four ways."

"Four?" Stokes said. "Riders and train and dynamite. That's only three."

"They got artillery," Raider replied. "Some cannons. They couldn't get the mortar across the lake. Hey, where'd you get this flyer?"

"Nagadoches."

"Word's goin' out all over." Raider frowned, shaking his head. "Why the hell do they wanna kill Hayes?"

Stokes hunkered down next to Raider. "Well, I tend to follow the events of our nation. I must read a newspaper at least once a week. Sometimes every day. I like to . . ."

"You gonna jaw or you gonna tell me somethin' that might help?"

"Okay, Mr. Smarty Britches," Stokes huffed, "just this: Hayes has been pullin' the last of the reconstruction troops out of Louisiana. And these boys might be comin' at it from two sides."

"Which two sides would that be?"

Stokes pointed at Raider. "Shut up and I'll tell you."

"Good way to lose a finger, Stokes."

"You wanna hear this?"

Raider nodded, fighting back his irritation with Stokes's slow manner.

"All right," the paunchy man said. "This boy that wired you up to the cross. He thinks he can start trouble by ambushing Rutherford B. Hayes himself. Maybe get the war goin' again."

"He cain't."

Stokes agreed. "Any sane man could figure that out. But judgin' from this spook show I saw, these boys ain't sane."

"Holt is," Raider said. "He's got somethin' else in mind."

"He the one who put that train over yonder?"

"Yep."

Stokes rubbed his chin. "Well, the railroad's been doin' a lot of business with the army. Maybe they don't want the rest of the troops to go either. They might be losin' money."

It made sense to the big man. "Holt somehow gets hooked

up with Starbin. He plays t' the ol' rebel's sense o' pride. Starbin had money an' he was able t' stage that robbery up in Dallas. Shit."

"What?"

Raider pointed toward his feet. "You gotta pop these blisters, Henry. Then you gotta wrap my feet for me."

Stokes chortled cynically. "When did I get elected to be your momma?"

"This ain't no time to quibble, Henry. You gotta do it 'cause I know you'll do it right. Then we can get after those on the other side o' the lake. Hell, we got four days."

"Two days," Stokes replied. "I heard it from the man who gave me the flyer. Hayes has moved his speakin' up till the thirteenth. Today's the eleventh. Anyhow you look at it, it's two days."

"Shit, Henry, you gotta fix my feet. I ain't as good at doctorin' as you are."

"How you know I'm good at doctorin'?"

"I heard," Raider replied.

Henry nodded as if it took great effort. "Okay, you Arkansas madman, I'll fix your feet. But what about the woman?"

Raider thought about it for a moment. "Hey, I know a guy on the other side o' the lake who'd love t' stay here an' take care of a pretty woman. We'll have t' go that way anyway. Boy's name is Gus."

Stokes was eyeing him in a strange way.

"What's eatin' you, Henry?"

"You said *we* got to get after those boys. I thought you never worked with partners."

"We're ass-deep in Indian grass, Henry. The way I see it, I ain't got much choice."

Stokes bristled. "Well, who said I wanted to work with you anyways?"

"Well, do you?"

The short man with the paunch seemed resigned to a fate worse than death. "All right, Raider, I'll work with you. But just this once. You hear me? Just this once."

The big man from Arkansas said that was perfectly all right with him.

CHAPTER NINETEEN

The east Texas sun was beginning to peek over Raider's right shoulder as the big man pulled at the oars. Cool morning air raised fog on the smooth surface of the black water. Henry Stokes sat behind Raider, straining to peer around him. Stokes didn't look too happy.

Raider turned to gauge his direction. He was looking for the creek that led up to the railroad compound he had seen ten days earlier. It had taken them the whole night to rig out and to make sure Regina was taken care of.

Stokes hadn't seemed overly found of Gus, the swamp rat. "You sure that old boy'll take care of that pretty woman?"

"Yeah."

"I mean, what if he tries somethin' on her?" Stokes offered.

"He won't. He'll be more int'rested in the liquor cabinet."

"Raider . . ."

"Shut up, Henry."

Stokes bristled, but he shut up.

Raider glanced over his shoulder again, straining to see through the mist. Things were so still that anybody in the compound would hear the oarlocks grinding. He lifted one oar and gave it to Henry.

"Paddle. Quiet-like."

Stokes obeyed, remembering all those stories about how Raider wouldn't work with a partner because the big man's partners were always being killed. One kid hadn't even lasted a month. Henry wondered how long he would last. He kept dipping the paddle in the water, looking anxiously into the fog.

Raider wheeled around, paddling with his eyes forward.

He hoped old Gus would make it back to Regina. The poor woman had cried and begged him not to leave her alone. Raider had little choice in the matter. He had to stop Holt and Starbin from killing President Rutherford B. Hayes.

"There it is," Stokes said.

Raider saw it too; the entrance to the creek. "You got good eyes, Henry."

The big man listened but he could not hear a thing. No train whistle, no roar from a forge, no hammer on iron. Maybe Starbin had already left. He wondered if any sentries had remained behind to guard the compound.

"Go straight in?" Stokes asked.

Raider nodded. "But not up the creek. We'll ditch this tub on the bank an' walk the rest o' the way."

They pulled the ragged rowboat up on the shore.

Raider hesitated but he heard nothing in the still air.

He led Stokes toward the well-packed trail he had been on before. There was no guard to meet them, so they moved straight down the trail through the shadows of the morning. Everything was quieter than an Indian burial ground.

Raider clutched a .38 Diamondback in his hand, the kind his old partner used to carry. Raider had liked the weapon so much, he had purchased one for himself. The chubby man in the derby carried his own cannon, a Dutch four barrel scatter-gun loaded with the biggest buckshot he could find.

They paused when they saw the opening ahead of them.

Not a peep.

"They're gone," Raider said.

"Didn't leave nobody behind?" Stokes wondered.

Raider shrugged. "Why should they? Come on, let's have a look."

Together, the two Pinkertons moved out into the compound. Quickly they examined the work stations: the forge, the anvil, the gunsmith, the shop where they had worked on the artillery. All the wood in the camp was gone, no doubt transferred to the engine for kindling and fuel. Everything else had been left in place, like the men planned to come back to the camp.

"Raider, look at this."

Stokes was waving from a small shed at the far end of the compound.

Raider hurried over to look into the hovel. "Lord A'mighty!"

Stacked in the shed were large piles of currency; dollar bills in large denominations. Raider picked up a bundle and lifted it into the light. The ink was still wet on the paper.

"Fake," he said.

Stokes nodded. "There's a printing press right there. I reckon Starbin wants to print his own money once he takes over the . . ."

A rifle echoed in the stillness. Splinters of wood shattered on the wall of the shed. Raider and Stokes both hit the ground, crawling low as the rifle kept on talking to them.

When they were on the safe side of the shed, the rifle stopped.

Raider tried to look around toward the direction of the shots. "Did you see where he was?"

As Stokes shook his head, the rifle went off again, shattering a big chunk of wood next to Raider's head.

The big man drew back in one piece. "Damn, I reckon we woke 'im up when we got near that bogus money."

Stokes took off his derby and put it on the barrel of his scattergun. "Here; when I give the word, stick this out."

Raider scowled at him. "What good is that gonna do?"

"Just do it. Okay?"

Stokes slid over to the other side of the shed. "Okay, now!"

Raider stuck the hat out and the rifle responded accordingly. The slug nipped the brim of Stokes's derby. Raider pulled the scattergun back.

"I got him marked," Stokes said.

Raider offered him his hat.

"Hell," the paunchy man replied, "you didn't have to let him shoot a hole in it, Raider!"

"Let me get a shot at 'im."

"Out of range," Stokes said. "Here, give me my shotgun and I'll go see if he needs a new asshole."

"What?"

"I'll shoot him another one," the little man rejoined.

Raider started to protest, but Stokes left in a hurry, running for the stretch of forest behind him. To cover him, Raider eased the Diamondback around the corner and fired off a couple of shots. The rifle replied in kind.

"Damn that Georgia cracker."

But he held tight, waiting. Every few minutes, he would fire once or twice to keep the rifleman honest. Had to be only one, otherwise they would have closed in already.

What if Stokes didn't come back? Another dead partner. Raider wondered if maybe he had better get moving. Somebody had to get to Shreveport to warn President Hayes, to stop the wild attempt on his life. What the hell were they hoping to do by killing Hayes?

Raider flinched when the cannon sound of four shotgun barrels rolled through the air. The big man knew he could stand up now. He walked around the corner of the shed to see Stokes coming straight for him. He held the scattergun, still smoking in his hand.

"He hear you comin'?" Raider asked.

Stokes shook his head. "We got to go, big 'un."

"I know. Any horses around?"

Stokes gestured toward the railroad tracks. "There's a handcar. You know how it works?"

"Like a seesaw," Raider replied. "Two of us gotta pump up an' down. I'd druther have a horse, though."

"Yeah, me too. Come on. We're probably too late anyway."

"Prob'ly," Raider replied. "But we gotta get up the line an' send a message to Shreveport."

Stokes agreed that was their best bet.

Raider stopped pumping the handcar when he saw the engine on the tracks ahead of them. His heart skipped a couple of beats. His hand reached down for his pistol. At first he thought the engine might belong to Starbin, but then he remembered that the death train had a boxcar attached to it.

Stokes wheeled around to look at the engine. He had not expected to hit something so soon. They had only been pumping for a couple of hours.

A grey haired man looked out from the cabin of the engine as they pulled up. He waved, like he was expecting them. Raider and Stokes wielded their weapons when they leaped off the handcar.

"Hey," the grey haired man said, "take whatever you want but don't kill me, please."

"We're Pinkerton agents," Raider said. "Lookin' for a train that musta come this way last night."

"I'm just an engineer," the man replied. "I ain't seen it."

Stokes waved the barrel of his scattergun. "Then tell me this, mister engineer. How come you're sittin' right here on this track where it come through? The *only* track, as far as I can see."

The engineer shrugged. "There's a track up ahead connects with this one. I had to back down here because another train is due through Tenaha in a few minutes. Then I go back there to head for Austin."

Stokes looked at Raider.

The big man nodded. "Makes sense. Unless he's workin' for Starbin."

"Name's Screeney," the engineer said. "Ain't workin' for nobody but the East Texas Rail Company."

Raider lowered the Diamondback and looked up the track. "You say Tenaha is ahead. They got a wire there?"

Screeney nodded.

"We can send a telegram to Shreveport," Stokes offered.

"Wire don't go that far," Screeney replied.

Raider slipped the Diamondback into his belt. "Don't matter. We can get a wire out to somebody who can get to Shreveport."

He started to climb into the engineer's cab.

"Hold on," Screeney said, "In the name of the East Texas Rail Company, I can't allow you to board my train without permission."

Stokes showed him the shotgun. "This is all the permission we need, mister. Now move aside."

"You say you're Pinkertons," the engineer said. "So if you are, you have to abide by the law."

Raider shook his head. "You don't understand, sir. I don't have time t' tell you all the details, but let's leave it at this. Then if you don't wanna help us, I'll back off."

"Say your piece."

"A gang o' men is on the way to Shreveport t' kill President Rutherford B. Hayes. An' me an' this boy here has gotta stop 'em." Raider held out his hands. "Now, is that good 'nough for you?"

Screeney thought about it for a moment and then said, "One of you boys is gonna have to shovel coal."

"Good," Raider replied. "I volunteer . . . Stokes."

"The hell you say!" the paunchy man rejoined.

They took turns until the engine was moving toward Tenaha. They barely got up a head of steam before Screeney had to throttle down. Raider went to send the message out to the nearest town, which was Grand Bayou, Louisiana. He also sent a wire in care of the home office in Chicago, as well as a wire to the offices of the governors of Texas and Louisiana. Somebody had to sit up and take notice. Another message to Grand Bayou asked the local law enforcement officials to stop the train.

When he came out of the wire office, the other train was passing, heading west for Austin. Raider lied to the engineer and told him that he had garnered permission of East Texas Rail to use the train for Pinkerton purposes. Best that the old gent thought he was doing right by his bosses. Raider figured to square things later, if there was trouble.

"We'll need more coal and water to catch them," Screeney offered.

Raider glared at the railman. "You think we can catch up?"

Screeney shrugged. "Maybe. I was talking to the station attendant. That rig ahead of us is an old one. And he's pullin' a car. I might be able to gain on him enough to catch him before tomorrow, providing he stops along the way."

Raider clapped him on the back. "Okay, Screeney, let's get movin'."

The big man shoveled coal for a long time before he handed the shovel to Stokes. They helped Screeney as best they could as he piloted the lone engine through the night. Raider even managed a nap right before dawn. The whistle awakened him just outside Grand Bayou.

Stokes and Screeney were staring ahead, toward the carnage that lay scattered over the small village.

"Jesus help 'em," Raider muttered. "They killed the whole town."

CHAPTER TWENTY

Raider and Stokes didn't take long to piece together the events that had taken place in Grand Bayou. Apparently the message about the death train had preceded Starbin and his bizarre band of men. Some of the townsfolk had taken the message seriously and tried to gather a posse to stop the train. The attempt had been in good faith, but Starbin's crew had been too much for them.

"Look at the hoofprints," Stokes said, gesturing to the ground. "The horsemen got out to finish the job."

Raider sighed. "I bet they didn't even get off the messages I sent 'em."

He turned to the engineer. "Screeney, we gotta go. You ready t' cover some ground?"

The engineer nodded but he looked worried. "We got to turn the train north," he said. "Some of them dead people on the track will have to be moved."

Raider didn't want to make light of the massacre, but he knew more damage would be done if they didn't get to Shreveport. "Stokes an' I will move 'em."

Stokes grimaced even though he knew it had to be done. "Wish we had time to bury them all."

"Later," the big man replied. "After we finish in Shreveport."

In Wallace Bayou, Screeney stopped the engine long enough to learn that a train decorated with red, white, and blue streamers had passed through the small town just hours earlier. The train had a banner on it that said, "Welcome President Hayes." It was very festive and everyone in Wallace Bayou had waved as it passed.

"They better thank God they didn't pull iron," Stokes said.

Raider jumped back into the cab with them. "Screeney, can we get this thing t' go any faster?"

"Maybe if we took on more wood," the engineer replied.

"Then do it."

Stokes wiped his forehead with the back of his hand. "We ain't gonna make it," the paunchy man offered.

"Mebbe not," Raider replied. "What time is the president s'posed t' give his speech?"

Stokes shrugged. "Four o'clock. But you know how that goes. Them things is always late."

"What time is it now?"

Stokes pulled a pocket watch from his trouser pocket. "Ten after three."

"How far is Shreveport?" he asked the engineer.

"Hour, maybe hour and a quarter."

Raider pointed a finger at Screeney. "One hour. I'm gonna hold you to it, you hear."

"Hell, then," Screeney said, smiling nervously. "Make it fifty-nine minutes."

"Sold," Raider replied.

He just wondered if it would be enough.

One hour and twenty minutes later, Raider could see the crowd that had gathered to hear President Hayes. He didn't know if the president was speaking yet. But he could see Starbin's train parked ahead of them. It was visible from a quarter mile away. Raider recognized the plated walls of the black boxcar, the one that contained a nest of rifle-toting hornets. Did they plan to kill everybody at the rally, the same way they had killed the whole town of Grand Bayou?

Stokes came up beside him. "Is that it?"

Raider nodded. "We made it."

"Did we?"

Screeney asked if he should throttle down.

Raider was about to say yes when two doors opened on the black boxcar. Four riders leaped out into the crowd. The people had been applauding something. The entrance of the President of the United States?

"Son of a bitch," the big man said, "they've set it in motion."

"What are we going to do?" Stokes asked.

Screeney said that he had better start to throttle down before they rammed into the other train.

Raider stopped him from reaching for the throttle. "Speed up," he commanded. "Give it all the steam we got left."

"But we'll crash!" Stokes said.

"That's what I want," the big man replied. "It'll take ever'body's mind off the president."

The riders had begun to circle, just like they had done in training.

Some shots were fired.

Screams from the crowd.

Screeney blew the whistle on his engine, hoping it would help to disperse the spectators.

"Jump before we hit," Raider said.

Stokes was glaring at him. "So this is how you get me killed!"

"Just jump, boy!"

Screeney tied down the throttle and nodded.

They all three leaped at the same time, landing knee-deep in soft mud as the train went forward.

Raider could still hear shots as he struggled to get out of the mud.

"You better thank God it rained here this mornin'!" Stokes cried from the mire.

He was about to say something else when the noise of the crash drowned out his voice.

As crashing metal and wooden shards exploded in the air, Raider just stood there helplessly, watching as one edge of the crowd seemed to be cut down by a reaper's blade. The ones who were hit scattered as quickly as they could. Some of them ran straight into the paths of the four riders who barreled down toward the platform where the president had been scheduled to speak. Was Hayes still alive?

Raider started toward the center of the melee.

Stokes called to him, telling him to wait. It was suicide to run into that mess. But Raider kept on, knowing that he had to stop the four riders before they did any more damage.

The big man looked up to see one of the horsemen coming straight for him. Raider raised the Diamondback and aimed carefully. When he squeezed the trigger, the rider fell out of the saddle.

Raider managed to swing onto the mount as it ran by him. When he was up over the crowd, he was able to see the riders better. One of them got off a rifle shot in his direction.

Reflexively, the tall Pinkerton reached for the scabbard on the saddle's sling ring. His hand found the wooden stock of a '73 Winchester. He lifted it and cut down the man who had been firing at him.

Two more.

They swung over, hanging low on the other side of their mounts. Raider couldn't fire low without hitting some of the fleeing spectators. They pushed against his mount as well.

Best just to ride low like his adversaries. They were heading for the speaking platform. And the big man thought for damn sure they were going to make it . . .

Henry Stokes pulled himself and the engineer out of the mud.

When he turned back to the crowd, he stood there calmly, wondering if anyone was going to try to run over him. But they all seemed to be heading away from the burning train.

Henry left the engineer to climb back onto the track. He gazed down at the twisted wreckage, thinking that all those stories about Raider's destruction were true. At least *he* was still alive to tell the tale.

He started toward the burning mass of wood and steel. He figured all of the riflemen in the boxcar had been killed without getting off a shot. Probably the conductor of the train and anybody else inside it had died as well. He couldn't help thinking how lucky he was to be alive.

When the heat from the crash became too great, Stokes stopped to survey the crowd again. They were still running headlong in every direction. He picked out the horsemen right away, including Raider.

Stokes lowered his eyes a little to see something else that he had not expected. Two men were calmly unfolding a red, white, and blue canvas tarp. They were uncovering a small cannon that had been primed.

Stokes fumbled for his derringer inside his coat pocket. "No! You bastards."

The cannon was aimed at the speaker's platform. Stokes fired the derringer but he was nowhere close to hitting his mark. The cannon exploded when one of the men put a match to the proper hole in the body of the weapon. A whistling sound seemed to rise and fall. Then the charge exploded, landing squarely in the middle of the President's lectern.

Being far away from the platform saved Raider's life. The two riders he was chasing were not as fortunate. The explosion from the cannonball cut them down in an instant. Raider felt the force of the erupting charge but he still managed to stay in the saddle.

When his mount's front hooves were on the ground again, he wheeled and charged straight for the two cannon men, who made the mistake of running toward Stokes. The paunchy little man reached inside his coat for a larger weapon, a Remington .44 revolver that was hidden in a secret pocket. He had to shoot one of the cannon men to get the other to surrender without a fight. Raider rode up as Stokes was tying his prisoner.

"I couldn't stop them before they set off that big gun," Stokes said.

Raider looked back toward the platform, which was now burning as badly as the train. "Think the president is dead?"

Stokes nodded toward the platform. "Why don't you go have a look?"

The crowd had scattered, making it easy for the big man to ride slowly toward the flames.

Was Hayes there when the cannonball went off?

Maybe they had made enough ruckus beforehand to head him off.

The flames were flickering high toward the sky. Raider rode in a wide circle, looking for signs of life. Nothing moved in there. There were bodies scattered all around. Was one of those corpses the President of the United States?

A numbness set in on him. He rode back toward Stokes, refusing to look down at the ground. Too many people had been killed and some of it had been his fault. Hell, would it have been any different if he had let Starbin's men do their job? Either way there would have been killing.

Stokes wasn't there on the tracks when Raider got back.

Maybe he was on the other side of the railbed. Maybe he couldn't stand the sight of it any more than Raider. He had to wonder if Starbin and Holt were in the train when the engine smashed into it. If they weren't, somebody had to find them and bring them to justice.

"Stokes!"

He urged his mount up onto the tracks.

Suddenly rifle levers began to chortle and men rose up from the other side of the track, aiming straight at Raider's head.

They had taken Stokes captive.

A man in a white suit climbed onto the track, taking the reins away from Raider. "Don't try it, cowboy. You aren't that good."

"Who the hell are you?"

"I'm John Donahue, United States Department of the Treasury. And you're in a hell of a lot of trouble, cowboy."

"Can we talk 'bout this someplace else?" Raider asked. "Maybe where there's a bottle o' whiskey?"

Donahue replied that they could talk about it right here, right now and without the whiskey.

CHAPTER TWENTY-ONE

Raider sat on the railroad tracks with his chin in his hands. All around him lay the carnage that he had single-handedly bestowed on the gathering at Shreveport. Well, maybe not quite single-handedly, but the way it was starting to look, the big man seemed to be getting all the credit for the pandemonium that had ensued with the train wreck and the cannon shot. He wondered how long it would take the locals to clear it up and forget about the whole thing.

John Donahue, the government man, had been listening to Raider for the better part of an hour, trying to find holes in his story. Donahue was a good agent; the big man could tell. Donahue asked the right questions, probed the right sore spots, paid attention to the pertinent details. Raider felt it was a shame that Donahue didn't believe him, otherwise they might have become friends or associates.

Donahue shook his head, rubbing his cheek with his fingers. "You mean to tell me that you're working for the state of Texas? Trying to stop some sort of plot?"

Raider exhaled, throwing out his hands. "I told you, this man named Clay Forbin hired me t' look into somethin' that was goin' on in East Texas. Forbin was from the state attorney's office, but a man named Holt had 'im killed. If you'll just wire the governor or my agency. . ."

"You don't look like a Pinkerton," Donahue interjected. "Nor does your colleague there."

Raider was almost ready to give up, but he kept on anyway. "We're troubleshooters," he replied. "Forbin went all the way t' Chicago t' ask the agency boss t' get on this thing. And this man Starbin was in on the plot t' kill the president. He was stealin' in Texas. Where d' you think that cannon came from?"

Something flashed in Donahue's brown eyes. "Do you have any idea of the whereabouts of this man named Starbin? Or Holt?"

Raider pointed to the burning train. "If they ain't in there, they musta' got off somewhere along the route. Probably runnin' back t' their hole right now. A rat always runs back t' his hole."

Raider shuddered when he thought that Starbin and Holt might be heading to Zavalla. Regina was there with Gus. When the mad pair of murderers discovered that Regina had survived . . . he didn't want to consider it further.

"Something wrong?" Donahue asked.

Raider shook his head. "No. Just somebody who'll prob'ly die if you don't turn me loose t' go find Holt an' Starbin."

"So you don't think they're in the wreck there?"

"Gen'rals don't always ride into battle with their troops."

Donahue frowned. "Explain yourself."

"Like I told you afore, this Starbin an' his daddy have some sorta plan t' make the Confederacy strong again. They look at ever'thin' like it's the army. Captain this, private that. Bond Starbin got 'is legs an' 'is pecker blown off in the war so he's pretty steamed up about it."

"And Holt?"

Raider's eyes narrowed. "He's got somethin' t' do over here, on the Louisiana side o' the border. Somethin' with trains or such. I don't know. I get the feelin' he's hooked up with some pretty big people."

One of Donahue's men scoffed, shaking his head. "These boys ain't Pinks, Mr. Donahue. Look at 'em."

Raider glared back at the man and he stopped smirking. "Look, I hadta infiltrate that gang in Texas. Didn't you see the riders? They was headin' straight for the President. I hadta look like this so they'd think I was one of 'em. Holt also framed me for the murder of Forbin. I'm wanted over in Texas, which don't help me none here, but it's the truth. I'm tellin' you the truth all the way, Donahue. If you don't b'lieve me . . ."

Donahue reached into his coat pocket and produced a picture that he handed to Raider. "Is this the man you knew as Holt?"

Raider gaped at the likeness. "That's him. Hey, where'd you get this? An' what're you boys doin' here anyway?"

Donahue snatched the picture out of his hand. "We were sent here to smoke out this very man. Only his name is not Holt. It's Rivera. Celio Rivera. Or at least that was the name he used when he commissioned this train from the rail company."

"Prob'ly got a lot o' names," Raider offered.

Donahue put the picture back in his coat pocket. "When he commissioned the train, he paid for it partially with counterfeit money. That's when I was called in. The Department of the Treasury was asked to look into this matter because such a large amount of fake money showed up."

Raider glanced at Stokes. "Just like those bogus bills we found over in Texas," he said.

Stokes nodded. "Looks like these boys was comin' at it from the other side, Raider. And we met in the middle."

Raider smiled. "Reckon that's it."

Donahue wheeled around, pointing a finger at him. "You're damned right we were coming at it from the other direction. And you charge in just as we're closing the net around this train. You ruined everything."

"Whoops."

Stokes looked at Donahue. "Well, is the President all right at least?"

"There's no president here," Donahue replied. "Mr. Hayes is back in Washington, safe and sound. This whole rally was a ruse to draw out the men who were planning to assassinate him. Thanks to you, we weren't able to stop anything."

Raider felt a pair of aces dropping into his hand. "Now, hold on," he started, "them riders was in motion before you boys moved in. And you couldn'ta been too close, otherwise that train crash would'a killed you. Hell, I stopped that train load o' boys an' cut down a couple o' the riders while y'all were somewhere playin' pocket billiards."

"People were killed," Donahue insisted.

"I'm sorry 'bout that," Raider replied. "But people would've been killed even if I hadn't caused that crash. An' I don't wanna hear any more o' this shit 'bout how great a job y'all were doin'."

"What are you getting at?"

"Just this," the big man replied. "Y'all didn't have no idea that train was loaded t' kill. I stopped it for you. An' most o' the gang is dead, 'ceptin' for the leaders."

Another of Donahue's men said, "You don't have to take that, boss."

Donahue sighed. "Yes, I do. This man is right. We had no idea that train was carrying men with guns or horsemen to storm the platform. And we might have been killed in the melee, had we tried to fight it out with them."

Raider straightened up, looking hopeful. "Now you're talkin', chief. You gotta let me go, so I can find Starbin an' Holt."

"Not so fast," the agent replied. "First, I want to send wires to the Pinkerton agency and then to the governor's office in Texas."

Stokes asked if he could reach into his coat. When Donahue nodded, he produced his own Pinkerton credentials. Donahue took a look and then tossed them back to Stokes.

"What's it gonna be?" Raider asked.

"You can go," Donahue replied.

Several of his men protested.

Donahue shot them a stern glance. "If this man is telling the truth, and I have every reason to believe he is, then he's the only one who can catch up to the perpetrators. He knows them and their methods."

"That's it," Raider rejoined enthusiastically. "That's the whole damned truth, Mr. Donahue."

The agent gazed back at one of his men. "Simpson, give him your rifle and your sidearm."

"But Mr. Donahue . . ."

"Just do it."

The man handed Raider a '76 Winchester and a Colt .45. "I'll see that you get these back, Simpson. Or if I don't, you'll be paid."

"Take that horse you were riding," Donahue offered. "Do you need any money?"

"Whatever you can spare."

Donahue tossed him a five dollar gold piece. "I want a report when you've captured them. And I intend to check out your story."

Raider pointed to Stokes. "What 'bout him?"

"He stays," Donahue replied.

"Aw, hell," Stokes said. "Raider's gonna need my help."

Donahue scowled at the paunchy man. "Do you think I'm crazy? If I let one man go that's one thing. But I caught two of you and I'll need some insurance, in case you aren't telling the truth."

Raider rested the barrel of the '76 on his shoulder. "We're tellin' the truth, mister. But you can hold Stokes. An' don't worry, he ain't feelin' sick. He just looks that way 'cause he's from Georgia."

They watched as Raider swung into the saddle and turned the horse south. He spurred the animal forward, wondering if he would be able to catch Holt and Starbin. They probably got off the train at Grand Bayou, after the big slaughter. That meant they had a head start on the big man.

But Raider possessed a talent for making up time on the trail. It was one of his strong points. And he was going to need them all if he planned to finish the East Texas conspiracy.

After riding through the night without a single clue, Raider arrived in Tenaha the next morning. He stopped at the wire office again to send a message to Chicago. He had forgotten that everyone in the next town had been killed by Starbin's men. When the key operator told him the line was dead into Grand Bayou, Raider hung his head.

"What is it?" the operator asked.

Raider shook it off. "Nothin'. Nothin' but killin'."

The operator snorted disgustedly. "Had some of that around here last night."

The big man glanced up. "Where?"

"Out back," the telegraph man replied. "Heard shots when it was pitch black. Two of them. Had to ride out at dawn to see what it was. Found a couple of dead men."

"You notify the sheriff?"

"No sheriff in Tenaha. We got a marshal that comes through once in a while. Every so often a Ranger. I get robbed now and then, but we just can't afford to pay no lawman."

"What are you gonna do with the bodies?" Raider asked.

"Just wait for the marshal, I reckon. 'Course, I could put 'em on a train that's comin' through, but that might not be for a couple of days."

Raider squinted, peering into the man's eyes. "I want a look at those bodies, pardner."

The operator grimaced. "You what?"

"I'm a Pinkerton agent, on the trail of three men who might've been headed this way."

"Mister, I can't allow it. I'm responsible."

"Then answer me this," the big man said. "Was one o' the bodies missin' a couple o' legs?"

The man frowned. "I don't . . ."

"You really didn't bring in them bodies yourself, did you?"

The operator lowered his eyes. "Okay, it wasn't me. I was actin' big, tryin' to impress you."

"Where are they? The bodies, I mean."

The operator pointed across the street, to the livery. "Our blacksmith has 'em under straw and lye, over behind the stable."

"Much obliged, pardner. And don't feel so sorry about actin' big. It happens t' all of us once in a while."

The operator nodded dolefully.

Raider crossed the street and made a deal with the blacksmith. He would have his horse shod if the smithy would let him look at the bodies. It sounded sort of strange to the smithy, but he agreed as he needed the business.

The big man from Arkansas didn't have to look very close at the corpses.

"Funny, ain't it," the smithy said. "The old man wearin' a rebel uniform and the other one not havin' any legs."

"Yeah, funny," Raider replied blankly.

Holt or Rivera or whoever he was had killed his partners in cold blood.

"Shot in the back," the smithy offered.

Raider asked if the livery had a fast horse he could trade for. He was going to need a fresh animal if he planned to catch up to Holt. He knew the dapper outlaw was heading for Zavalla, back to Starbin's spread and Regina.

When the blacksmith named his terms, Raider agreed without a hitch. In fifteen minutes, he was saddled up, heading south, following the railroad tracks. A rat always returned to its hole. And Peter Holt, alias Celio Rivera, was certainly a rat.

CHAPTER TWENTY-TWO

The bodies of the Starbins were just the beginning. Peter Holt left a wide trail that made Raider wonder if Holt knew somebody was on his tail. He was moving quickly too, barely evading Raider at every turn. Was he really that lucky? Or that smart?

When he conducted a search on the compound in the woods, Raider discovered that Holt had taken most of the counterfeit money from the printing shed.

Down by the creek, the big man found three sets of prints in the soft, muddy bank. Holt had paid the swamp men—with the fake cash, probably—to take him across the lake. The mud hadn't even seeped far into their tracks. Holt was probably already with Regina, hurting her.

Raider looked back at his mount, a tall chestnut gelding that still seemed pretty fresh. "You like t' swim, boy?"

Using one of the flatboats, Raider pushed off, holding the reins of the chestnut. He poled the boat down the creek, leading the horse straight into the water. The animal waded until the bottom dropped out and then he started to swim.

Raider hoped his mount could make it all the way across the lake. He didn't want to leave it behind. What if Holt had already fled? There probably weren't any horses at Starbin's place. They had all been used in the raid.

Maybe Holt had planned his escape as carefully as he had planned the incident in Shreveport.

He would head south, Raider thought.

The horse whinnied behind the flatboat when they reached the lake. It shook its head, rocking the narrow craft, almost plunging Raider into the dark water. He pulled the reins and the gelding settled into a crawl, swimming faithfully behind the swiftly moving vessel.

Holt wasn't at Starbin's place.

Raider searched the house but came up with very little. At least Regina had gone without a fight. Holt had made her pack a bag. He was going to head for the water, Raider thought. He wouldn't go north, or back to Austin. He'd go to Beaumont or Port Arthur.

As he mounted up for the ride, Raider caught a shape out of the corner of his eye. Old Gus, the swamp rat, was lying dead next to the house. Shot in the back. Raider didn't feel too good about that turn of fortune. Even though he couldn't spare the time, he had to bury Gus before he left.

"Too damned much dyin' on this one," he said as he patted the dirt mound.

He climbed back into the saddle, wheeling south.

Holt wouldn't go north to Dallas, not after the robbery at the armory there. Austin was out because the local constables had Holt fixed as one of the suspects in Forbin's murder. South, to Beaumont or Port Arthur.

He spurred the chestnut, which seemed to be fresh again. He'd have to stop for a couple of hours at least. No need to kill the poor animal. Maybe he could pick up a train along the way.

When he heard the whistle blowing at dusk, he knew he had a chance to catch up with the dapper fugitive.

In Beaumont, Fernandez was helpful. He had no real loyalty to anyone, so he spoke freely about seeing Holt, even though he was sure that Raider was no longer an outlaw.

"Rivera, that's what I called him. He's in Port Arthur. Said something about hiring a steamer to take him to Florida."

"Florida?"

Fernandez nodded, draining a shotglass full of good whiskey. "There's a little fishing town there. Tampa. He's going there."

"When's he leavin' Port Arthur?"

Fernandez shrugged. "Who knows? Two days, a week."

Raider started to get up from the table.

The man in the sombrero called to him. "Hey!"

Raider turned to see Fernandez rising out of his chair. He

slammed the shotglass on the table. "Señor, I have heard that you are a very fast gun. Faster than me."

"Try it," the big man said.

Fernandez moved for his gun.

Before he could lift it halfway, Raider had drawn the .45 from his belt, fanning back the trigger.

Fernandez laughed and dropped his gun back into his holster. "Thank you for not killin' me, pardner."

Raider backed away from him. "Don't mention it, Fernandez. An' thanks for tellin' me 'bout Holt. I mean Rivera."

"Port Arthur," said the smiling man in the sombrero, "you can make it by tomorrow morning."

In the tiny gulfside town of Port Arthur, Raider had no trouble finding the only outgoing steamer. It was a big, two-wheeled job that was bound for New Orleans, not Florida. Raider watched it for the better part of the day before he saw Peter Holt and Regina Starbin as they strolled along the deck. Holt had a strong grip on her. Regina looked sad but healthy. At least he hadn't been beating her.

After they disappeared into their cabin, Raider stopped an old rummy who was passing by on the docks. "Pardner, what's that boat there?"

"*Texan Queen*," the rummy replied. "Headin' for Loozieanna. Say, you wouldn't have a nickel for a pint, would you?"

Raider held up a silver dollar. "You can have this if you tell me a lot more."

The man licked his dry lips. "Well, I do know that a man done chartered her for a trip around the gulf. All by hisself with his wife. Paid cash. Hired his own crew. Still lookin' for a boiler man."

Raider straightened up. "Yeah? When's she plannin' t' leave?"

"Tonight. In a couple of hours."

Raider tossed him the silver dollar. "Here, go drink your head off."

The man thanked him and hurried away.

It took Raider a couple of hours to complete the disguise. He found clothes worn by a working man, a ship's boiler mate. A floppy hat hid most of his face. When he approached the captain of the *Texan Queen*, the big man was totally convincing.

"Get down to the boiler room at once!" the captain said. "Get me some steam. I got one other mate on this tub and he's lazy as can be."

Raider took a few minutes to find the boiler room. He had been in the guts of a steamer several times, on a few occasions with his former partner, Doc Weatherbee. Doc had shown him how to run a boiler. He just hoped he could remember it all.

The fire was glowing but it wasn't very hot. Raider tossed in some kindling which ignited immediately. He followed with more wood and some coal. Something hissed behind him. He turned to look at a safety valve. Spin the red wheel. Wasn't that it?

A big gauge rested next to the valve. The needle was in the red. Raider turned the wheel clockwise. The needle eased back into the black zone.

A whistle blew next to him. The captain's voice boomed down a tube "Not that much steam, you lubber! Now, throw the shaft. I want to get out with the tide. You hear me? Throw it!"

Raider tried the levers behind him. He pushed all of them down at once. There was a grinding noise, but then the boat began to move. The captain called down again, telling him to keep the fires hot.

"Son of a bitch," the big man said. "I did it."

Outside, he could hear the paddles splashing in the water.

They were sailing, so he had to move quick. Find Regina and get the hell back to dry land. He could handle things. After all, it was only Holt and a couple of crewmen. Once he got the woman free, he could play it as it came.

Reaching into his seabag, he withdrew the .45 given to him by Donahue.

As he was turning for the hatch, the red wheel caught his eye. Something Doc had done once before. It had made the whole ship blow up. That might just be what he had to do. End it once and for all. Holt had escaped the train wreck in Shreveport, but now he was going to get his due.

Raider moved slowly along the deck, trying to stay in the evening shadows. Somebody groaned ahead of him. He stopped and waited for the lazy crewman to walk by. Raider just grabbed the lad and threw him overboard, into the drink. They were close enough for him to swim back to the dock.

And his cries could not be heard over the noise of the paddle-wheels.

Raider figured swimming a piece was better than getting blown up. He'd have to find a way to get the captain out of his wheelhouse. After all, the skipper did not deserve to die, just because he was hired by Holt.

Slipping quietly forward, Raider eased into the wheel-house, holding his .45 on the old salt. "Steady there, Captain. Don't move."

The captain's eyes widened. "Hey, I didn't mean to be so cross with you, mate. No need for revenge."

"It's not like that," Raider said. "You gotta abandon ship. I'm gonna fry your employer before he gets away."

"You're daft, man. I've got to guide this boat through Sea Rim, until we're clear to the gulf."

Raider hesitated. "Okay. But if you see me go overboard, you better foller in a hurry. You got that?"

The captain looked scared. "Listen, there's no reason to destroy my ship. Take Rivera, hang him for all I care. I'll cooperate if you're some kind of law."

"Pinkerton agent."

"Then go get him."

Raider sighed. "Okay, I'm trustin' you. I hope it don't come to it, but I may have t' do it anyway. Besides, did you know Rivera paid you with fake money? He printed it his-self."

"That's right, I did, Captain."

Raider turned to see Holt, alias Rivera, stepping out of the shadows. He had come through a small door at the back of the wheelhouse. He held a shotgun in his hand.

"How admirable," Holt said. "You found me. And you escaped our little trap. You have persistence, Raider."

The big man remembered the red wheel he had turned. He cast a glance toward the pressure gauge by the Captain's post. The needle was inching toward the red. Raider just smiled.

Holt waved the barrel of the scattergun. "Drop your weapon."

Raider nodded toward the steering wheel. "I shut off your steam, Peter. Or is it Celio? Which one killed the Starbin boys?"

"There's plenty of steam," Holt said. "Am I not right, Captain?"

The old salt's eyes bulged when he looked at the gauge. "My God!"

He threw a lever that made the boat lurch, rocking in the water.

As Holt fell off balance, Raider lunged for the doorway, rolling out onto the deck. Quickly he ran for the cabin door where he had seen Regina and Holt together. His boot splintered the jamb with one kick. Regina lay on the floor, having fallen from the boat's sudden movement.

"Raider, is it really you?"

He picked her up. "Come on, honey. We ain't got but a few seconds."

As they ran back out on deck, Holt's shotgun exploded. The pellets flew over their heads. Raider leaped onto the rail, pulling Regina with him, and sailed overboard without a moment of hesitation. It stung when they hit the cold water, but he figured it was better than going down with the ship.

They both treaded water, bobbing in the wake of the steamer.

Regina wrapped an arm around his shoulder.

"Easy, girl."

"Can we swim all the way back to shore?" she wondered.

Raider paddled around until he was looking in the direction of the departing vessel. He thought he saw somebody else leap off the deck. Probably the captain, who realized the boiler was about to blow.

Holt was running back and forth on the deck for a few moments before he went back into the wheelhouse.

He was steering the vessel when the boiler exploded.

The flames lit up the evening, the sound echoed over the bay.

Raider and Regina felt the explosion in the water.

The fireball had no doubt been seen from shore.

Within minutes, the *Texan Queen* had sunk swiftly into the bay, hissing and steaming as it went down.

Large pieces of debris were floating all over. Raider grabbed something to hang onto and Regina grabbed him. They drifted for a while before the tide swept them up onto shore. They were frozen, shattered, but alive.

Collapsing in the sand, they held each other for warmth until the sun began to rise . . .

CHAPTER TWENTY-THREE

They managed to walk far enough to find a man with a small boat. The man was going across the bay anyway, so he said he would take them for free if Raider helped with the rowing. The big man agreed, wondering if he looked like something God would throw in His trash bin. Regina didn't seem so bad. maybe she had gotten used to misfortune.

The boatman was an oyster peddler. All the way over on the crossing, he extolled the virtues of the tasty shellfish. When he mentioned their aphrodisiac qualities, Raider offered to try a few. He almost gagged on them.

"Just not for your taste," the man offered.

Raider kept rowing.

Regina had a tight hold on his legs.

"Wrap your head in something," Raider said.

She looked up pitifully. "Why?"

"I don't want you to be recognized in Port Arthur. They'll remember a beautiful redhead. I don't want 'em t' see your hair."

She smiled slightly. "Beautiful?"

"Yes, you are," Raider said.

"Yes, she is," the oyster dealer replied. "Would you like to try one, miss?"

Regina said she would pass.

The talk in Port Arthur was of the explosion in the bay. It had rocked the little community, but as horrible as it was, it still held a fascination for the citizens. So nobody noticed Raider and Regina as they headed for the livery to pick up Raider's mount.

Riding double, they started out of Port Arthur, undetected by the rest of the populace.

Raider wondered if the wanted poster of him was still in circulation. It might yet be trouble. Best to keep moving if he wanted to get back to Starbin's place. Somehow, he felt things would be all right if he could get Regina back there.

Fortunately, his rifle was still in the scabbard on his sling ring. He could shoot a few meals, make camp with his bedroll. They slept side by side, touching but going no further. Neither of them wanted it just now, but it felt good not to sleep alone.

"You're a sweet man, Raider," she told him the next morning.

They mounted up again and headed north.

When they got to Starbin's place that afternoon, they saw that Stokes was waiting for them.

He was cooking dinner in the kitchen.

When Raider walked in, the pudgy agent barely looked away from the stewpot.

He just sipped the stew gravy and nonchalantly told Raider that he had a lot of news.

After Regina had eaten and then retired to her bedroom, Stokes and Raider sat down at the table with a bottle of good Kentucky whiskey.

"Yeah," Stokes started after the first drink, "I sat there until all the telegrams came back. Donahue was finally convinced we was tellin' the truth. By the way, did you catch Holt?"

Raider shrugged. "Kinda."

"He's dead, ain't he?"

Raider nodded. "Yeah."

Stokes shrugged. "So what? You can send a report to Donahue. And the old man's gonna want one too. Hey, did you destroy anything?"

"A steamship."

"Well, let's hope the steamer company has insurance. The rail company did and you're in the clear over that crashed train. Hell, the governor of Louisiana even gave us a commendation. I hope you won't mind that I accepted it for both of us."

Raider said he didn't mind. "You got any news about my wanted poster?" he asked Stokes. "Am I still a criminal?"

"Nope. The governor of Texas fixed all of that up. You're free and clear on that charge. Let's hope you're as lucky about the ship."

Raider looked down at his glass of whiskey. "Nobody knows I set off the explosion. 'Ceptin' for that captain and I ain't even sure he made it outta the wreckage."

Stokes rubbed his chin, thinking. "Hmm, I could say that the suspect was killed in an accident," he offered. "In my report to the agency I mean. I can say whatever you want."

"Tell the truth," Raider replied. "Or anything you want."

Stokes said he'd take care of it.

Raider shook his head sadly. "I don't know, Stokes. I'm sorry 'bout all those people who was killed."

"Grand Bayou couldn't be helped," the paunchy man replied. "They tried to stop that train. Maybe we shouldn't have told them to, but they made the choice to try. As for the rally, most of them that was killed belonged to Starbin's little band of soldiers. Only a few of the other spectators were killed. Some were done in by that cannonball, but all in all only about twenty people were found dead."

Raider sighed. "Well, I reckon it's over."

"Not quite, Mr. Pinkerton!"

The call had come from the back porch.

Raider and Stokes froze as Peter Holt eased into the house. He was holding a shotgun. "Don't move, either of you."

"How the hell did you get here?"

"Do you think you're the only one who can swim? Why I . . . argh . . ."

Holt tensed, his face contorting in hellish agony. He turned slightly but never got to face the woman who stabbed him in the back with a hayfork. Holt took a couple of steps forward, falling face first onto the floor. Regina Starbin hovered over him as the life ran out of his body.

"I saw him sneaking around," she said softly. "From my window. I went out the front door and followed him. When he came in here, I picked up that fork. I don't know, it wasn't like I was doing it. I'm afraid, Raider."

He put his arm around her. "Come on, honey. Let's go upstairs."

Stokes's face turned red. "Damn, he gets the woman and I get to bury another body."

"Shut up, Henry. Cain't you see this young lady is frightened?"

Upstairs, they held each other tightly. But it wasn't like the trail. Suddenly they both found they wanted it to happen. Raider was hard and Regina was wet. He rolled over and slipped into her, shaking the bed until they were both too tired to move.

CHAPTER TWENTY-FOUR

William Wagner had been keeping an eye on the mail ever since Henry Stokes sent him a telegram that stated a full report would follow. Wagner wondered how Raider would look from another perspective. Stokes had a tendency to tell the whole truth, to hold nothing back. Raider always wrote one or two sentences unless he dictated his reports to someone. Even then the details of a case got lost.

So when the envelope finally arrived, Wagner opened it, hastily reading Stokes's concise hand. Stokes told of the plots on both sides of the Texas/Louisiana border, how Holt had masterminded the scheme to kill the President. He went on to tell how it was all wrapped up, how Wagner should have gotten the reports from the various government agencies, from the rail company, from the Department of the Treasury. Wagner balked at the part about Holt's steamer "accidentally" blowing up. That had Raider's mark all over it.

"William, what's got you so rapt in your work?"

Allan Pinkerton was standing in his doorway.

Wagner held up the report from Stokes. "The east Texas affair. Stokes sent the final tally."

"And the damages?"

Wagner eyed the fourth paragraph. "Nothing really. Except for the lives of many people."

Pinkerton sighed. "God bless their souls."

"We may end up being responsible for the loss of a steamship, but I'll have to wait and see what happens."

"Any more word from Raider and Stokes?"

Wagner shook his head. "Nothing in here, either. I received that last wire from Zavalla saying that they were going to take a few weeks off. But nothing since then."

Pinkerton shrugged. "For once, I think the big galoot has earned himself a rest. What was that about the steamship again?"

"I think Raider blew one up to get his quarry. It says here that the man named Holt disappeared after his steamer burned. That was Raider's doing if I don't miss my guess."

"And you probably don't miss," Pinkerton replied. "Let's wait. Maybe it will all blow over."

Wagner held up another stack of wires and letters. "I've heard from the governors of Texas and Louisiana, the East Texas Railroad, the United States Department of the Treasury and a telegraph operator in Tenaha, Texas. They're all saying that Raider saved the day."

"I suppose he did," Pinkerton said, turning back into his office.

Wagner tossed the papers back on his desk, gazing toward the big window that looked out onto Fifth Avenue. It would be Christmas Day very soon. A light snow had been falling all week, covering the ground with a layer of white. A wonderful time of year, especially when your wildest agent had just solved an unbelievable case.

Stokes had helped him too, making Wagner wonder if he should risk pairing them again. No, he decided, looking at the report. Stokes was too valuable. Raider had almost gotten him killed this time. Best not to risk it again.

He looked up at the window again, thinking it was time for him to find a Christmas tree.

EPILOGUE

The buckboard wagon bounced in another chuckhole.

"Damn," Henry Stokes wailed, "are you gonna hit every bump in the road, Raider? It's hard on my back."

Raider shook the reins of the wagon, urging the two horses to speed up. "You know, Henry, I didn't ask you t' come with us. I asked Regina here an' you just invited yourself along."

"Regina said I could come," Stokes replied. "Didn't you, Miss Regina?"

She was perched on the buckboard seat next to Raider. "Now, now, you boys don't fight. Why, this is Christmas Eve and we're almost to Raider's uncle's house. You don't want to spoil it by fighting, do you?"

Raider smiled at her. "That's right, honey. Now you hush up, Henry. Otherwise Santy Claws ain't gonna bring you nothin'."

"I hate Arkansas," Stokes muttered under his breath.

What he really hated was the fact that the pretty woman preferred Raider over him. But that couldn't be helped. Stokes had never been much of a ladies' man. Even if he still liked to look at them, they never responded much in kind.

"I'm so happy," Regina said, crooking her arm in Raider's.

The big man just smiled, knowing she would be on a train east, back to her people, after they spent Christmas with Raider's family. It had only taken them a few days to sell the old Starbin place and cash in her assets. After all, she had inherited everything after the death of her husband. She was now a woman of means.

"This was a lovely idea, Raider," she said.

"Lovely," Stokes mocked in a high voice.

They had been sitting around the kitchen table when the

notion struck them. Raider wasn't far from Arkansas, where his uncle and aunt had a farm. Since Regina didn't have any kin nearby, she suggested that they travel to Ouachita to see Raider's uncle. Stokes said that was a good idea. Before Raider could tell him he wasn't invited, Regina said Stokes should come along.

So they caught the stage in Nagadoches, riding all the way to Little Rock where they rented the buckboard.

The ride had been bumpy, but they were almost there.

Stokes kept nipping at his little bottle of whiskey.

"Pass some of that up here," Raider said.

"Only if you let me drive," Stokes replied.

The big man pulled back on the reins. "Okay."

He switched places with Stokes.

Regina went with him.

Stokes huffed his disappointment. "I don't never get the girl."

"Just hush up and drive," Raider said, sipping the whiskey.

Regina snuggled up to the big man, taking a sip herself. "You shouldn't be so hard on him, honey."

Raider smiled. "Aw, he's just mad cause he don't have nobody to cuddle with. I'll fix 'im up with Elvira Bradshaw when we get home. She's ugly an' desperate enough t' go for Henry."

"I heard that!" the paunchy man cried.

"So you don't want to meet Elvira?" Regina offered.

Stokes snorted. "Didn't say yes or no."

Raider and Regina laughed until Stokes joined them.

"Pass that whiskey back up here, you Arkansas galoot."

Raider gave up the bottle and pulled Regina closer. "I'll take you to Texarkana when we're finished here," he said. "You can catch the train there. That's what you want, ain't it?"

She looked sad for a moment, but then smiled weakly. "I know you ain't the kind of man to stay very long with a woman. But I owe you a lot. And I think I love you."

"Here that, Stokes? She loves me."

Regina slapped him playfully. "Oh, you!"

The cold air seemed to close around them toward dusk.

Regina dozed off and Raider wasn't too far behind her.

They both woke up when Stokes pulled back on the reins.

"Raider, I think we're here. It's just like you described it. Hey, look, it's startin' to snow."

Raider rose to peer down into the valley. He could see his uncle's cabin in the distance. The fire was glowing inside. Lamps were also burning. The house seemed to be full of people.

"Take 'er down, Henry. All the way to the door."

His uncle gaped for a moment when he saw the big man. "Ray?"

His aunt and his cousins were all sitting around the fire.

"Is it really Ray?"

"Yeah, and he's got his friends with him."

Raider gestured to the man and the woman behind him. "This is Henry Stokes and Regina Starbin. I said they could spend Christmas with us."

Uncle Jess smiled warmly. "Welcome home, Ray. And your friends are as welcome here as family."

Henry Stokes took off his hat. "Much obliged, sir. Would you like a snort of some Christmas cheer?"

"Think I will," Raider's uncle replied.

Aunt Hannah took Regina's arm. "My, my, you are pretty, aren't you? Are you Ray's girl?"

The big man grimaced. "Aw, Aunt Hannah . . ."

The two women disappeared into the kitchen.

Raider grinned at his cousin. "Hello, Johnny. What's Santy Claws gonna bring you?"

"A rifle I hope!"

Raider knew he had a squirrel gun in the wagon for the boy. He wanted it to be a surprise in the morning. He stepped next to the fire, warming his hands. It felt good to be home for a change. Home for Christmas with his family. Somehow it made everything hurt a lot less. A whole lot less.